NEW YORK REVIEW BOOKS
CLASSICS

FATALE

JEAN-PATRICK MANCHETTE (1942–1995) was a genre-redefining French crime novelist, screenwriter, critic, and translator. Born in Marseille to a family of relatively modest means, Manchette grew up in a southwestern suburb of Paris, where he wrote from an early age. While a student of English literature at the Sorbonne, he contributed articles to the newspaper *La Voix Communiste* and became active in the national students' union. In 1961 he married, and with his wife, Mélissa began translating American crime fiction—he would go on to translate the works of such writers as Donald Westlake, Ross Thomas, and Margaret Millar, often for Gallimard's *Série noire*. Throughout the 1960s Manchette supported himself with various jobs, writing television scripts, screenplays, young-adult books, and film novelizations. In 1971 he published his first novel, a collaboration with Jean-Pierre Bastid, and embarked on his literary career in earnest, producing ten subsequent works over the course of the next two decades and establishing a new genre of French novel, the *néo-polar* (distinguished from the traditional detective novel, or *polar*, by its political engagement and social radicalism). During the 1980s, Manchette published celebrated translations of Alan Moore's *Watchmen* graphic novels for a *bandes-dessinée* publishing house co-founded by his son, Doug Headline. In addition to *Fatale*, Manchette's novels *Three to Kill* and *The Prone Gunman*, as well as Jacques Tardi's graphic-novel adaptations of them (titled *West Coast Blues* and *Like a Sniper Lining Up His Shot*, respectively), are available in English.

DONALD NICHOLSON-SMITH's translations of noir fiction include Manchette's *Three to Kill*, Thierry Jonquet's *Mygale* (a.k.a.

Tarantula), and (with Alyson Waters) Yasmina Khadra's *Cousin K*. He has also translated works by Guy Debord, Paco Ignacio Taibo II, Henri Lefebvre, Antonin Artaud, and Guillaume Apollinaire. Born in Manchester, England, he is a longtime resident of New York City.

JEAN ECHENOZ is a prominent French novelist, many of whose works have been translated into English, among them *Chopin's Move* (1989), *Big Blondes* (1995), and most recently *Ravel* (2008) and *Running* (2009).

FATALE

JEAN-PATRICK MANCHETTE

Translated from the French by
DONALD NICHOLSON-SMITH

Afterword by
JEAN ECHENOZ

NEW YORK REVIEW BOOKS

New York

THIS IS A NEW YORK REVIEW BOOK
PUBLISHED BY THE NEW YORK REVIEW OF BOOKS
435 Hudson Street, New York, NY 10014
www.nyrb.com

The translator wishes to thank Robert Chasse, Doug Headline, Mia Rublowska, and Alyson W. Waters for their precious assistance.

Copyright © 1977, 1996 by Éditions Gallimard, Paris
Translation copyright © 2011 by Donald Nicholson-Smith
Afterword copyright © by Jean Echenoz
All rights reserved.

Cet ouvrage publié dans le cadre du programme d'aide à la publication bénéficie du soutien du Ministère des Affaires Etrangères et du Service Culturel de l'Ambassade de France représenté aux Etats-Unis.

This work, published as part of a program of aid for publication, received support from the French Ministry of Foreign Affairs and the Cultural Service of the French Embassy in the United States.

Library of Congress Cataloging-in-Publication Data
Manchette, Jean-Patrick, 1942–1995.
  [Fatale. English]
 Fatale / by Jean-Patrick Manchette ; introduction by Jean Echenoz ; translated by Donald Nicholson-Smith.
    p. cm. — (New York Review Books classics)
 ISBN 978-1-59017-381-7 (alk. paper)
 I. Nicholson-Smith, Donald. II. Title.
 PQ2673.A452F313 2011
 843'.914—dc22

                              2010034848

ISBN 978-1-59017-381-7

Printed in the United States of America on acid-free paper.
10 9 8 7 6 5 4 3 2 1

To my beloved

I

THE HUNTERS were six in number, men mostly fifty or older, but also two younger ones with sarcastic expressions. They all wore check shirts, sheepskin jackets, waterproof khaki trench coats, more or less high boots, and caps. One of the two younger guys was all skin and bone, and one of the fifty-year-olds, a bespectacled pharmacist with white hair in a crew cut, was fairly thin. The other hunters were potbellied and rubicund, especially one named Roucart. They carried two- or three-round sporting guns because birds were the game. They had three dogs, two pointers and a Gordon setter. Off to the northeast there must have been other hunters because they heard a gunshot, followed by another, from a kilometer or perhaps a kilometer and a half away.

They reached the end of a stretch of damp moorland. For ten meters or so they passed through silver-birch saplings barely taller than a man, then they found themselves amidst large rustling trees, mainly birch and poplar, and thickets. The group loosened. There was standing water here and there. From the northeast came four or five more distant reports, a muted crackle of fire. A little later they broke up deliberately. They had been hunting for a good three hours and still had not killed anything. Everyone was frustrated and crotchety.

A moment came when Roucart went down into a damp, narrow coomb strewn with masses of rotting leaves. He found the descent rather hard because his paunch pulled him forward and he was obliged to dig in his heels and throw his head back. His head was shaped like a pear, stem upwards, and his bald pate was red beneath his green-and-brown camouflage-style cap. The skin of his face was red too, his eyes bright blue and his eyebrows white. His nose was short and stubby, with wide nostrils and white hairs inside them. He pulled up at the bottom of the coomb to catch his breath. He propped his gun against a tree trunk, then leaned back against it himself. Mechanically, he felt in his jacket pocket for a cigarette, then recalled that he had given up smoking three weeks earlier and let his hand fall to his side. He was disappointed. Suddenly a gunshot rang out no more than a hundred meters away and a badly trained dog barked briefly. Roucart had no dog. Without removing his considerable backside from the tree trunk, he leaned forward and with his mouth half open cocked an ear in the direction of the sound. All he heard at first was the murmur of the leaves, then someone coming down behind him into the coomb. He turned his head with some difficulty to see a young woman standing motionless at the foot of the incline, just four steps from him, a thin figure in a long light-brown oilskin, waders, a round rain hat over her long brown hair. Slung over her shoulder was a 16-gauge shotgun.

"Good heavens! If it isn't Mélanie Horst!" exclaimed Roucart, hastily detaching his rump from the tree trunk and sucking in his stomach. "Well, this *is* a nice surprise! But how come? I thought you had left us for good, dear child."

She smiled vaguely. She might have been thirty, or thirty-five. She had dark brown eyes and delicate features. The vague smile barely exposed her teeth, which were small and even. Roucart approached the young woman, continuing to address her as "dear child" and talking in an avuncular tone as his big blue eyes roved up and down her slim form. He declared himself greatly astonished to see her here—first because she never went shooting and secondly because she had said her goodbyes to everyone the previous afternoon and taken a taxi to the station.

"As surprises go, this beats all. And such a pleasant one too," he exclaimed, and she unslung her 16-gauge shotgun, turned it on him, and before he had finished smiling emptied both barrels into his gut.

Moments later he was lying on his back against the upward slope and its rotting leaves. His torso was full of holes and his khaki jacket had ridden up beneath his chin from the impact and his check shirt was half out of his pants. Roucart's bare head was bent forward and twisted to one side, his cheek was in the mud, his eyes and mouth were open, and his cap lay upturned on the ground. With saliva glistening in his mouth, the man narrowed one eye slightly and died. From far away there came the sound of three gunshots. The young woman walked away.

2

IT WAS night when she went into the station, and she had reversed her oilskin, which was light brown on one side and white on the side now visible. A red scarf was tied around her brown hair and the frame of her large glasses was black-and-white check. The young woman's mouth was at present made up with scarlet lipstick. The station was hardly crowded. An Arab family with three children waited on a bench, peeling oranges. Lamplighters were going to and fro with oilcans suspended from their belts. The young woman made her way to the self-service luggage lockers. Opening a locker at one end of the row, she took out a slim attaché case and a large leather bag. Then, going to the other end, she opened another locker and removed a green plastic briefcase with a zipper running around three sides. She slid the fastener open about twenty centimeters and looked quickly inside the case, which was twisted and bulging from the volume of its contents. Raising her head, she zipped it up again. With her three pieces of baggage, she went and sat down in a corner of the station hall and smoked two Celtiques.

After ten or twelve minutes a royal-blue luxury train pulled into the station. By this time the young woman was already on her way to the underground passage. She emerged onto the platform just as the train came to a halt. She walked for fifty meters or so alongside the train, checking the car numbers. She came to her sleeping car. A porter greeted her on the platform and took her ticket, along with the leather bag and the slim attaché case. She kept the overstuffed briefcase under her left arm and grasped its edge with her right hand as she climbed into the carriage and made her way to her single sleeping compartment. The porter set the bags down. He told the young woman that they would arrive at Bléville* at eight o'clock the next morning and asked whether she would like a wake-up call. At seven, she replied. Smiling, she asked the man whether it would be at all possible to bend the rules and deliver a meal to her compartment, a meal whose desired components she detailed. The porter began by saying no, but then fell prey to the charm of her smile and the fifty-franc bill she held out to him, folded in half and nipped between two fingers. All the while she barely took her eyes off the briefcase, which she had put down on the made-up bunk.

When the porter returned a good while later, only her reading light was on and the young woman was almost naked. A towel worn turban-fashion was tied low on her forehead, while her body was covered by another, rather large towel pulled tight below her armpits, leaving her shoulders and arms bare and falling to her heels like an African woman's *pagne*. The porter placed the food on the little table, uncorked one of the two bottles of champagne, and placed their silver-plated ice buckets on the floor, saying it would be best if she called for him when the second bottle needed opening. Then, after she had paid him with bills extracted from a black box-calf billfold, he swiftly withdrew.

The train had been back in motion now for about fifteen minutes, often approaching a speed of one hundred and eighty kilometers per hour. Once the porter left, the young woman turned all the lights in the compartment back on. She removed the towel from her head and her hair appeared, still very wet and streaked yellow and black. The little towel was badly soiled with black dye. Bending over the washbasin, the young woman rinsed the remaining black dye from her hair. From her large traveling bag she took a small hair dryer. Earlier she had set on the floor an American battery-powered hair-setting device designed to heat twenty rollers, and turned it on. She plugged the dryer into a socket by the washbasin and dried her

---

*Bléville is, literally, Wheatville, but *blé* in a slang sense means money. The town's name is thus something like Doughville.—*Trans.*

hair. Thanks to a reversible chemical change, the red core of the rollers had turned black, indicating that they had reached the desired temperature and were ready for use. The young woman, blonde now, threw off the large towel, which was hindering her movements. She rolled her hair into the twenty curlers. She pulled the edge of the lowered blind aside slightly. She got a vague impression of night rushing by and of dark masses that were copses or buildings. Here and there lights could be seen in the distance. Occasionally an illuminated railroad crossing shot past, close by the train. She let the blind fall back and went to sit at the little table. She reached out and picked up the briefcase. She put it on her lap and unzipped it completely. Carefully she counted the five-hundred-franc and hundred-franc notes that it contained. From time to time she dropped one, and the tips of her breasts would brush against the money on her knees as she leant down to retrieve the fallen bill. In all, the briefcase surrendered some twenty-five or thirty thousand francs; the young woman put the notes back, rezipped the case, and placed it on the floor next to the compartment wall.

Next she lifted the cover of the hot plate, revealing a choucroute. The young woman proceeded to stuff herself with pickled cabbage, sausage, and salt pork. She chewed with great chomps, fast and noisily. Juices dripped from the edge of her mouth. Sometimes a strand of sauerkraut would slip from her fork or from her mouth and fall to the floor or attach itself to her lower lip or her chin. The young woman's teeth were visible as she chewed because her lips were drawn back. She drank champagne. She finished the first bottle in short order. As she was opening the second, she pricked the fleshy part of a thumb with the wire fastening, and a tiny pearl of scarlet blood appeared. She guffawed, for she was already drunk, and sucked on her thumb and swallowed the blood.

She went on eating and drinking and progressively lost control of herself. She leaned over, still chewing, and opened the briefcase and pulled out fistfuls of banknotes and rubbed them against her sweat-streaked belly and against her breasts and her armpits and between her legs and behind her knees. Tears rolled down her cheeks even as she shook with silent laughter and kept masticating. She bent over to sniff the lukewarm choucroute, and she rubbed banknotes against her lips and teeth and raised her glass and dipped the tip of her nose in the champagne. And here in this luxury compartment of this luxury train her nostrils were assailed at once by the luxurious scent of the champagne and the foul odor of the filthy banknotes and the foul odor of the choucroute, which smelt like piss and sperm.

Nevertheless, when the young woman arrived in Bléville at eight o'clock that morning, she had retrieved all of her customary self-assurance.

3

WHEN SHE got off the train at Bléville, the young woman was blonde and her hair was as frizzy as a lamb's. She was wearing high boots in fawn leather with very high heels, a brown tweed skirt, a beige silk blouse, and a fawn suede car coat. On her right hand she wore two old rings with stones of no great market value and tarnished silver settings, on her left an engagement ring of white gold, and on her left wrist a small square Cartier watch with a leather strap. She hailed a porter and handed him her large traveling bag and her slim attaché case. She no longer held the green briefcase, but was now carrying a shoulder bag made of interwoven broad strips of beige and dark-brown leather. As she crossed the main hall of the station she glanced towards the bank of luggage lockers, which was impressively large.

In front of the station, the young woman handed the porter two francs and got into a taxi, a Peugeot 403. She told the driver to take her to the Résidence des Goélands—the Seagull Apartments. On the way she shivered and rolled up the window against the cold, damp sea breeze.

For her stay in Bléville, the young woman had chosen to call herself Aimée Joubert, and that is what I shall call her from now on. At the Seagull Apartments, Aimée Joubert's reservation had been duly noted. The girl at the reception desk, barely more than a kid at the awkward age, with acne and thoughtful, mean eyes, checked a register and then produced Aimée's keys and told her the floor and room number.

"You get two keys, okay?" she said as she handed them to Aimée.

"This is to the front door. It's locked after ten at night. We ask our guests to make as little noise as possible after ten. In the off-season, I mean. We have mostly elderly people here, and they like quiet."

"That's fine," replied Aimée. "I like quiet myself."

The girl did not show her to her room. Aimée carried her bags to the rear of the hall, took the elevator, and located her studio apartment on the fourth floor: a rather attractive room about twenty square meters in size, along with a wide balcony and a recessed kitchenette. An accordion-style sliding partition separated the cooking from the living area. There was also a narrow bathroom with a long tub and moss-green tiles. The furniture consisted of a double bed with a predominantly bright-red plaid spread, a bedside shelf with a telephone, a teak armoire, two easy chairs with blue velvet upholstery, a teak chest of six large drawers with brass handles, and a teak chair. The walls were white, the carpeting slate gray. In the center of each of three of the walls hung framed prints of eighteenth-century British ships of the line. A small Ducretet-Thomson television stood on the floor in front of the big picture window that took up the whole fourth side of the room. On the wide balcony were two more armchairs—garden chairs—and a round garden table, all in white-painted metal. The balcony overlooked the Promenade—a vast esplanade covered with yellowing grass and traversed by a pinkish roadway—and the choppy gray-green sea. All in all, fairly satisfactory lodgings.

Aimée unpacked and put away her clothes and other personal belongings, including a key-copying apparatus, a device for strengthening her hand muscles, and her chest expanders. Everything fit easily into the armoire. The young woman drew herself a bath. While the water was running she turned the television on, but nothing was being broadcast. She turned the set off and picked up a guidebook entitled *Bléville and Its Region* and a frilly clear-plastic shower cap. She pulled the cap over her hair and settled herself in the tub with the book. She opened the volume at random and began to read: *a whale, which in that millenarian period was believed to presage the end of the world....* (Aimée's lips moved slightly as she read.

She skipped a few lines; in any case the text had been familiar to her for some time.) *But it was the advent of oceangoing vessels that supplied the real basis of the town's wealth. The sons of Bléville proceeded to distinguish themselves in wars with first the English and later the Portuguese, and they ventured as far away as Canada and the East Indies. Under Louis XIV, trade and the* guerre de course *were the mother's milk of Bléville's prosperity. Following the decline of the port in the nineteenth century, the town was to wait until the 1960s for a new boom time to come. In those years the chemical and food-processing industries moved into the valley and the working-class suburbs underwent rapid expansion. Today Bléville can boast...* (Aimée broke off her reading at this point. On the facing page was a depiction of the same jetty and lighthouse that could be seen from her studio's balcony if one looked to the right.)

The young woman got out of the bath and used the handbasin to wash her tights, panties and bra with bar soap, then hung them up to dry on the chrome towel rack. She dressed in the same clothes she had worn on her arrival, except that she pulled a brown crew-neck sweater over her silk blouse. She left the apartment, put the keys in her bag, and went downstairs.

The streets of Bléville bore such names as Surcouf, Jean Bart, Duguay-Trouin, or alternatively such names as Turgot, Adolphe Thiers, Lyautey, and Charles de Gaulle.* Aimée walked up and down these streets for a while, occasionally consulting her guidebook, making sure that she was perfectly familiar with the town's topography. The young woman was almost exclusively interested, however, in the old town, dwelling place of the local bourgeoisie on the left bank of the river and well away from the port with its cafés overflowing with mussels and fries, with whores and seamen. To the rear of the affluent neighborhood quasi-expressways had made their

---

*Surcouf, Jean Bart, and Duguay-Trouin were celebrated French corsairs and admirals. Turgot was an eighteenth-century French statesman and economist; Thiers was known as the Butcher of the Paris Commune; General Lyautey fought in the French colonies and later became a Fascist.—*Trans.*

appearance, along with swaths of greenery and brand-new civic buildings adorned with abstract friezes. On the right bank a profusion of parallelepipedal dwellings with cream-colored rough-cast walls and tiled roofs bristling with television antennas spread up the hillside, their ranks interrupted by the occasional Radar, Carrefour, or Mammouth supermarket. Pushing eastward, and inland, one came to refineries, then to a plant producing canned fish, baby food, and cattle feed in three adjacent factory buildings, each operation bearing its own company name so as not to alarm consumers.

Aimée did not push eastward. In fact she took no more than a few steps on the right bank, venturing not far at all beyond the asphalted moving bridges that link the port and the inner docks. Neither the poor, the workers, nor their neighborhoods interested Aimée. It was the rich that interested her, and she went only where there was money. So she turned and went back over the bridges. At a newspaper shop she bought those national papers that gave space to small news items, as well as two local sheets, namely the *Dépêche de Bléville* and *Informations Blévilloises*. She thumbed through the Paris papers but failed to find what she was looking for. She turned to the local publications. One of them championed a left-capitalist ideology; the other championed a left-capitalist ideology. Both organs concerned themselves with the shipping news and reported on parish fairs, boule tournaments, minor car and motorcycle accidents, cattle fairs, and grain prices. In the *Dépêche*, a certain Dr. Claude Sinistrat railed in an opinion column about the pollution of the valley by L and L Enterprises. On this particular day the inauguration of a new covered fish market was announced for the late afternoon. Standing outside the newspaper shop, Aimée noted the names of several local luminaries and committed them to memory. Then she tossed both the local and the national newspapers into a wastebasket painted a garish green and bearing the legend KEEP YOUR TOWN CLEAN!

The young woman directed her steps toward the southwest part of the old town. Along the way she bought a Raleigh touring bicycle —heavy, expensive, and reliable—for the trips she was planning to make. She rode it to the offices, on the edge of old Bléville, of an attorney and realtor with whom she had made an appointment a month earlier under the name she was now using.

Maître Lindquist was tall and thin. He had large, dry hands, and large ears, and pale blue eyes in a long head with a balding pate the color of rare roast beef. He wore a black three-piece suit and a white cotton shirt and a loud green tie bearing a tiny red-and-gold coat of arms.

"I am so terribly sorry to hear that," he said when Aimée contrived to inform him that her husband had passed away. "I am a widower myself, so I know how you feel." He spread his hands and cocked his head. "And so you are thinking of moving to Bléville for the peace and quiet, of course. I can't see why that shouldn't be quite possible." He half smiled.

"Nor can I," said Aimée.

Lindquist looked at her a little stricken, hesitated, smiled, and cleared his throat. "You have no children, so the issue of school is moot. I feel sure we can find suitable properties for you to look at in the vicinity, by the sea—or there are charming villages around here, you know. Or right here in town. It all depends on how much you are looking to spend."

"That doesn't matter at all," said Aimée. "That's one thing at least I don't have to worry about. Just so long as the place is right."

"Yes, yes, I see." The realtor was visibly warming to Aimée.

"And the price has to be fair."

"Absolutely! Absolutely!" said Lindquist, wagging his head vigorously, his tone becoming even warmer, for he liked people who took money seriously.

Aimée added that she needed at least four rooms, and some land to ensure quiet, but that she had no wish to be isolated. She had been alone since the death of her poor husband, and it was time for that to end.

"Absolutely! Absolutely!" cried the realtor again, positively enthusiastic by this time.

"It's a sad thing, perhaps," said Aimée, "but it's only human: I am feeling the need to get involved in life again. Renew contact with other people. Make new friends."

"But my dear Madame Joubert," exclaimed Lindquist, "I feel sure you will make plenty of friends!" The man took his eyes off one of Aimée's knees that was exposed to view. "There is no shortage of excitement around here, you know." He hesitated. "We have fairs, we have the casino, we have...well, plenty of excitement!" He seemed to tire for a moment, but suddenly his features lit up once more. "Why," he exclaimed, "this very day we are opening the new fish market."

"How wonderful!" said Aimée. "Would you mind very much if I smoked in your office?"

"Not at all. Wait, perhaps you would care for one of mine?"

"Thank you, but no. I only smoke Virginia." Aimée produced a pack from her bag and placed a Dunhill between her lips.

The realtor was thinking what a charming little person she was, so fragile, so feminine, and he rose and leaned across the desk, emitting a tiny high-pitched grunt, unexpected and involuntary, as his muscles stretched; and he lit Aimée's cigarette with a silver table lighter in the form of an ancient urn.

"I shouldn't do this," said Aimée. "It's a vice. But you know what they say: the only reason we don't surrender completely to a vice is that we have so many others."

"Oh, really? They say that? How amusing! And indeed how true!" Lindquist smiled in a bemused way.

Eventually, once they had looked over the files of several properties for sale in the vicinity and arranged to visit one the very next day, the realtor warmly urged Aimée to attend the opening of the fish market a little later. The ceremony was to be followed by cocktails, and he would be delighted to introduce Aimée to some of Bléville's most eminent citizens.

4

AFTER leaving the real-estate office, Aimée rode back to her studio on her Raleigh along streets with such names as Kennedy, Churchill, and Wilson, and others called Magellan, Jacques Cartier, or Bougainville.* She stopped twice along the way, once at a pharmacy to check her weight on an automatic scale and once at a bookstore, where she bought a crime novel. In her clothes, she weighed 46.7 kilos. Without heels, she was 1.61 meters tall. On the scale was an enameled plaque bearing the message KEEP YOUR TOWN CLEAN!

As Aimée was going back to her studio apartment she noticed that a door some twenty meters farther down the corridor was ajar; peering out curiously from it was a little old lady, wearing a great deal of jewelry, who disappeared as Aimée entered her own room and closed herself in.

Once inside, Aimée drew the predominantly red plaid curtains and stripped naked. For nearly an hour she did exercises standing up and lying down on the floor, toning her muscles and making use in particular of her chest expanders. She streamed with sweat. She took out a thick piece of corkboard, placed it on the bed, and struck it repeatedly with the edge of first her right and then her left hand, likewise with each of her elbows. Setting aside the corkboard, she picked up a foam cylinder twenty centimeters long and twelve in diameter. Holding it in one hand, she adopted the lotus position. After a moment of relaxation, she kneaded it for a few minutes. Then, with both hands, she squeezed the cylinder tightly, reducing

---

*The last three were all renowned navigators and explorers.—*Trans.*

its diameter to just a few centimeters at the points where she was grasping it; she locked her muscles in this position and stayed quite still. A nervous twitch tugged at the sweaty skin at the corner of her mouth. Finally she put everything away and took a bath.

Lying in her hot bath, she opened the crime novel she had bought. She read ten pages. It took her six or seven minutes. She put the book down, masturbated, washed, and got out of the water. For a moment, in the bathroom mirror, she looked at her slim, seductive body. She dressed carefully; she aimed to please.

At four o'clock she left the Seagull Apartments and went shopping in the center of town for various items of clothing, all simple, all pretty, all rather expensive. She then proceeded to the Jules Ferry Leisure and Culture Center, on the east side of town, in the middle of a kind of municipal complex of recent vintage. There she signed up for fencing and Oriental martial-arts classes. She was directed to places where she could go to play golf, play tennis, ride horseback, and the like. Then, pedaling furiously, the young woman returned to her studio apartment and dropped off her purchases before leaving right away on foot, heading for the harbor, where the inauguration of the new fish market had already been under way for a few minutes.

Long and low, the gray cement structures of the market stood on a kind of peninsula flanked by two docking basins of unequal size. When Aimée arrived, a miniature throng had gathered at the entrance to the market precinct. From inside the market hall came bursts of monotone speech, then applause, and some of the folk outside applauded too, though not very loudly and not for very long. Aimée threaded her way through the knots of people peering inside with amused if not derisive looks. The people outside were poor, and odors of sweat and wine-laden breath rose into the brisk, briny, salubrious breeze.

The well-to-do were inside the building, or more accurately beneath a sort of immense curved awning overhanging the quayside. Two gloved policemen stood yawning at the entrance to the complex. They did not stop Aimée as she passed them and went under the immense awning. A platform had been set up in front of the cold-storage rooms, and on it a table with a large green canopy draped above. At the table sat middle-aged men in three-piece suits, with red faces and hair slick with lotion. In front of the table a local official, who had a little black mustache and was wearing pinstriped pants and a red-white-and-blue scarf, stood reading (or rather mumbling) a speech from five or six sheets of typescript.

"We have come together," this town worthy was saying, "to hail the dawn of a beautiful era! I have combed the archives of Bléville, gentlemen, and combed them thoroughly! And believe me, my dear fellow citizens, I had to go very far back in time before I found a record of a coming together, such as this one, of all the vital forces of Bléville in order to accomplish a task of general interest, a task capable of toppling the barriers of social class because it genuinely contributes to the prosperity of all, of workers, of business owners, of those in the service sector—all tightly bound together."

Aimée made her way through the scattered audience. She scanned the various groups and easily spotted Lindquist. She approached discreetly, not looking directly at him. He did not notice her. The place smelt of eau de cologne, tobacco, salt, and cement dust. There were few society women present. All the men wore ties except for three or four fish porters in freshly ironed shirts and cloth caps with large peaks. In a corner were twenty or so women workers in yellow blouses and little caps that made them look like nurses or exploited female labor in China. Lindquist suddenly recognized Aimée. Without hesitation he beckoned to her. She joined him. He introduced her to two couples who were with him, the Rougneux and the Tobies.

"Indeed I was obliged," said the worthy, "to go as far back as the sad year of 1871! In 1871 the Bléville chamber of commerce, whose centenary coincided—how could I forget it?—with the assumption of my own municipal duties, in 1871, I say, the chamber of commerce enthusiastically underwrote the construction..."

"Delighted, a great pleasure, how nice, how very nice to meet you," Aimée and the Rougneux and the Tobies were saying meanwhile, their forearms crisscrossing as hands were thrust forward for shaking. "Well, well, how very charming, do you play bridge? Yes? Ah ha! some new blood at last!" They went on for some time in this vein.

"...the construction of the old market hall," the worthy continued, "which today makes way in turn for this new hall in the center of which I stand at this very moment."

The Rougneux owned the bookstore where Aimée had bought her crime novel. The wife was thin and pale and wore a violet suit with a large gold brooch at the lapel and a string of cultured pearls around her neck. Her husband was thickset, the back of his neck close-shaven, his head large and cylindrical with a hairline low on his brow, and behind thick-lensed spectacles he had big glassy eyes. The Tobies were pharmacists, tall, thin, gray, and affable in a timid sort of way.

"Oh, look," said Lindquist to Aimée, "here is someone your age." And with that he introduced her to the senior manager Moutet, who had a good ten years on Aimée, sported a red mustache and a tobacco-brown suit, and worked at L and L Enterprises.

Aimée was far from bored. She distributed smiles; she offered opinions. Nobody was listening to the town worthy on the platform, who was now paying tribute to the New Fish Market Initiative Committee, whose members he named, beginning with Messrs. Lorque and Lenverguez of L and L Enterprises, and including M. Tobie, M. Rougneux, and M. Moutet.

"Nor should we forget these gentlemen's lovely wives," he added.

About ten meters from the group with whom Aimée was chatting, a guy of about thirty was looking at the young woman and smiling. He went on smiling as he came over to her.

"Sinistrat," he told Aimée. "Dr. Claude Sinistrat. Let me introduce myself, because I know that that old Huguenot is not going to do it."

"Oh, come off it, Sinistrat," said Lindquist.

"Delighted," said Aimée.

Sinistrat was tall and broad-shouldered, and by no means devoid of charm; his gestures were brusque and he had a big face, curly blond hair, and even teeth.

"I saw your opinion piece in the *Dépêche de Bléville*," said Aimée.

"I didn't pull any punches, did I?" Sinistrat puffed his chest out.

"Sinistrat," said Lindquist, "you are a scoundrel. And let me tell you—"

The realtor broke off. He was staring at something that his interlocutors could not see, somewhere in the crowd. He pursed his lips.

"Shit!" he exclaimed, and coming from him the profanity was startling. "Shit! That lunatic!"

The Rougneux, the Tobies, and senior manager Moutet all turned around at his words and scrutinized the crowd. Their attitudes bespoke anxiety and disgust. Aimée turned around too, her eyebrows slightly raised, and surveyed the gathering without seeing anything out of the ordinary. Sinistrat was all smiles. He lit a Craven A with a Zippo lighter.

"I don't see anything," said Mme Rougneux.

"No! No!" responded Lindquist. "He was there—outside."

"I don't see him."

"He's not there now. He must have gone off to plan more mischief."

"It's simply outrageous," said Rougneux. "I don't understand how they could have let him out. Those doctors are idiots. Their clinics are a joke." He spluttered after every sentence. He seemed mean, and pleased with himself.

"They are all drug addicts, leftists and that sort of thing," said Tobie.

"Next time they ought to put him in an asylum," said Mme Tobie.

"Be that as it may," said Sinistrat, "don't count on me to have him locked up."

"But my dear man," exclaimed Lindquist, irritated and contemptuous, "you might as well certify him as sane while you're about it."

"I'll consider it."

"What are you talking about?" asked Aimée.

Lindquist and the doctor turned towards her, both somewhat at a loss. For a moment neither said a word.

"Oh, nothing very interesting," said Lindquist.

"A little conflict," said Sinistrat with a slight flick of the hand.

"I love conflicts," said Aimée, but just then applause erupted, for the town worthy had concluded his speech and everyone was facing the platform.

Immediately after this, the talk turned to other things, and, leaving the *vin d'honneur* to the porters and small fry, the big fish repaired to the cocktail party they had arranged.

5

"THAT LITTLE doctor really has his nerve, it's unconscionable," said Lindquist as his sea-green Volvo slowly traversed the town with the realtor behind the wheel and Aimée seated at his side. The man shook his head. "Coming to the inauguration like that! And I bet you any money he'll be at the cocktail party too! He used to work at L and L, you know. The company doctor, or some such. They were obliged to let him go. And now he spews out his nonsense in the newspaper."

"He seems like a very rude man," said Aimée sweetly.

"He's a sort of nihilist," answered Lindquist. "He votes for that Trotskyite Krivine, you know."

"You don't say," answered Aimée.

"He's crazy," Lindquist explained in a definitive tone.

He parked the Volvo in a small triangular plaza. There was a fountain in the middle. The building façades on all three sides were cream and brown, with visible beams, or at least with illusory visible beams painted on them, and windows with little panes of thick glass and pots or planters of geraniums on their sills. One of the façades was that of a brasserie operating on two floors with its name, Grand Café de l'Anglais, painted in cream Gothic lettering on a brown background. Another was that of a private house, both halves of whose carriage entrance were open. There was much animation in the lobby, where two servants were relieving guests of their hats and coats. Lindquist and Aimée went through the hall and entered a large reception room crowded with people. A long trestle table had been set up, draped with a white cloth and set with a great many plates full of canapés. A white-jacketed server behind the table with his back to the wall busied himself with the spread.

There were about thirty people in the reception room. The women outnumbered the men. The Rougneux and the Tobies had already arrived. Just after Aimée and Lindquist, senior manager Moutet appeared with a voluptuous brunette. It was his wife. He introduced Aimée to her. The brunette Christiane Moutet had a vigorous handshake and a carnivorous smile and seemed at ease with herself.

"Do you play bridge?" she asked Aimée, and Aimée said yes. "At long last!" exclaimed the brunette delightedly. "We can never find a fourth who doesn't screw everything up."

"Oh, come on," said senior manager Moutet.

"Oh phooey!" said the woman. "Pardon my language."

Aimée smiled at her. Over the brunette's shoulder she saw that Dr. Sinistrat had arrived and was standing near the entrance accompanied by a petite young woman with short hair who was wearing slacks. The doctor appeared to be looking for someone in the crowd. The petite woman looked unhealthy and uncomfortable. Twice she covered an ear with the palm of her hand.

"Oh look, here come our hosts," said Lindquist, who was coming back from the buffet with flutes of champagne.

Aimée looked in the direction in which the realtor was pointing. At the far end of the reception room a group of people had just entered through a small side door: two men side by side, a woman just behind them, and another woman a couple of paces behind the first. Shaking hands and smiling, they made their way through guests filling up on sandwiches and champagne or whiskey and soda or vodka and orange juice. The woman at the back was a skinny blonde with pale eyes and long pale hair and hollows above the collarbone. She was wearing a shapeless pistachio-green dress adorned by a brooch set with rubies. Her eye caught Sinistrat's and veered away immediately; Sinistrat likewise averted his gaze. Aimée watched him. She took a step sideways, as though trying to keep her balance, so as to get closer to Sinistrat and the petite woman in slacks.

"My ears hurt," said the petite woman in slacks.

"Oh, give us a break, darling," said Sinistrat. "It's psychosomatic."

He wandered off towards the back of the room. Moments later, Aimée saw him talking to the pale-eyed blonde woman, smiling and handing her a glass of orange juice. Lindquist took Aimée's arm.

"Come, dear Madame Joubert," he said, "let me introduce Monsieur Lorque and Monsieur Lenverguez, the pillars of Bléville's prosperity."

"I'm just the man with the little jars," said Lorque.

He and Lenverguez were probably sixty years old. They were both stout. Lorque, the fatter of the pair, was very fat, with skin as smooth as a baby's and brownish eyelids and a gold chain on his royal-blue vest. Lenverguez was tall and stiff, with a crown of white hair, a strong nose and a severe gaze, beads of sweat on his brow, well-scrubbed fingers and nails square and manicured. Lorque and Lenverguez were smoking Havana cigars.

"Little jars?" asked Aimée.

"Little jars of baby food," replied Lorque. "Happy Baby baby food, Old Sea-Pilot canned goods, and L and L cattle feed—that's us." He looked pointedly at Aimée, teeth slightly exposed and head bent a little forward, as though he was saying something provocative. "He is the head," he added, digging Lenverguez in the ribs. "And I am the stomach. Better watch out. I swallow everything I touch."

"I won't let you touch me then," said Aimée.

"That's a good one," observed Lorque.

"Pay no attention to him," said the woman who was with the two men. "He loves to play the gangster."

"My wife," declared Lorque without turning his head.

Lenverguez looked around and shook his head.

"Where has mine gone?" he asked vaguely. He had a lisp and spoke rarely. He went off grumbling in search of the pale-eyed blonde, but she was no longer in the room. Nor, for that matter, was Dr. Sinistrat.

"Ah! Monseigneur!" cried Lorque suddenly.

Spreading his arms, he almost jostled Aimée in his haste to get to the entrance door, where a bishop had just appeared along with a young priest, both in business suits.

"He is a little bit nutty," observed Mme Lorque, smiling and following her husband with her eyes. "Do you play bridge, Madame Joubert?"

Christiane Moutet broke in to explain that she had already asked that question. Everyone burst out laughing. Everyone chattered. Sonia Lorque was affable, blonde, excessively thin, excessively tanned. Her white knitted dress set off her tan and her well-maintained body. She was a good twenty-five years younger than Lorque. One sensed that she took very good care of herself. Physically, she was like an aging starlet seeking desperately to preserve her beauty capital. That being said, she seemed neither highly strung nor stupid. She and Christiane Moutet invited Aimée to play bridge one day soon at the Moutets. Aimée accepted, then asked where she might powder her nose. They told her. She left the reception room and went up the grand staircase to the second floor. She was on the qui vive.

On the second floor was a long bronze-green hallway punctuated by white-painted doorways and reproductions of plates from the *Encyclopédie* of Diderot et al. depicting dock and industrial operations. No sound emerged from behind the white doors. Nor could anything be heard from the ground floor, thanks to the very thick walls and floors.

Near the door to the toilets was a settee with bronze-green upholstery. Aimée sat on it for a moment's pause. She needed a clear mind to process the information she had just acquired.

But at that instant Baron Jules emerged from the bathroom with his male member in his hand, crossed the corridor, and began to urinate against the wall just below an industrial print.

6

"FUCK! That feels good!" cried the baron once.

He had not seen Aimée, who was sitting motionless on the settee. The urine could be heard continuously battering the wallpaper. A dark puddle was forming on the bronze-green carpet between the two booted legs of this interloper. The man was tall, with a slight paunch, wearing jodhpurs and a brick-colored, roll-neck sweater that was too big for him and darned in several spots. He had a large pink head with a big nose and pale gray eyes and a tangled mass of graying platinum-blond hair. He must have been over fifty. He turned his head and saw Aimée.

"Hell's bells! A lady!" he remarked.

He turned towards her, still buttoning his fly.

"Let me introduce myself," he said. "Baron Jules. I must assure you that I am not in the habit of pissing on the floor in the presence of members of the fair sex. All hail beauty!" He shouted the last words. "Respect for the ladies!" He seemed to be calming down. "The fact is," he went on in a worldly tone, "that I have been holding it in since this morning, when I was released from the psychiatric clinic. I was saving it for the carpet of that fat Lorque, you see what I mean?"

Aimée nodded, nonplussed but hardly bothered.

"You don't see at all!" exclaimed Baron Jules. "You are a stranger to all this, and young! And very desirable, I might add, even though I prefer a little bit more flesh on the bone."

"Is that so?" said Aimée.

The baron smiled at her.

"YOU SHOULD EAT YOUR SOUP!" he shouted as loudly as he could.

Because of the noise, or by chance, the white door of a bedroom about ten meters away opened. Dr. Sinistrat and Mme Lenverguez looked out wide-eyed. They were holding hands. The hair of the blonde woman with the pale eyes was all awry and the doctor's tie was askew. The blonde's mouth formed an O and her face crinkled with embarrassment when she saw Aimée and the baron in the passageway. The baron smiled and bore down on the couple.

"Aha! Aha!" he whooped. "Adulterous little piglets!"

"Come now," said Sinistrat. "Come on, Baron, really..."

Mme Lenverguez emitted a mouselike squeak and fled for the stairs. Sinistrat stood his ground before the baron with arms bent and palms facing forward, as though seeking to halt, or merely perhaps to talk with him.

"Aha!" said the baron again with gleeful scorn. "She's in a funk. She's running away, the skinny bitch!"

"Baron Jules," said Sinistrat, "I must tell you—"

The baron grabbed the doctor by the lapels and shook him in a rather pacific way.

"You must tell me what, you little shit?"

"I must tell you that I'm not going to be pushed around anymore." Sinistrat's voice was quavering. He was breathing hard. "I'm not signing any more certificates so you can...go on cures—"

"And in exchange for that, you think you can count on my silence?" The baron headed for the staircase. "You stupid humanist!" he cried. "You are laughable." And the baron laughed a deliberate, forced laugh: "Ha! Ha! Ha! Ha!"

He disappeared. Mortified, Sinistrat sought to save face under Aimée's dispassionate gaze.

"He is mad," said the doctor. "He's completely—" He broke off. Then: "I must count on your discretion too," he added hastily.

Aimée shrugged, rose, and walked towards the stairs. Sinistrat followed in her footsteps, frantic. His curly hair flopped over his eyes and he tossed his head to get rid of it.

"That man is appalling," he was saying. "He pops up everywhere without being invited, and—"

"A priest! A priest!" The baron's voice thundered up from the ground floor.

"My God!" said Sinistrat.

With the doctor at her heels, Aimée quickly reached the bottom of the stairs. When she reentered the reception room, Baron Jules had just reached the bishop.

"Ugh!" he cried. "What an ugly priest he is!"

"My dear Baron, I beg you," began the bishop. He raised a pudgy hand, shaking his head and smiling, and the baron delivered a straight right to his jaw.

The bishop went down. Exclamations and horrified cries went up. People thrust themselves between the bishop and the baron, who was kicking at his victim and shouting that the black beetle should be left to croak. On the floor, the bishop was drooling. A very big guy in a striped suit, with a red ribbon on his lapel, a black mustache, and white teeth, grabbed the baron's arm and put him in a half-nelson.

"A cop! That's all we need," exclaimed the baron, stamping his heels onto the feet of the man with the mustache.

The bishop was helped to his feet and stood shaking his head in bewilderment. Lorque plonked himself in front of Baron Jules, jowls atremble with fury, and waved his Havana at him threateningly.

"You poor old fool," said the factory owner. "Nobody dares say it to your face, but I'll say it: You are not welcome here, you are not invited. You think you can do whatever you like because everyone in Bléville is afraid of you. Well, I'm not afraid of you." Lorque glanced at the man with the mustache. "Commissioner, throw this man out!"

"My pleasure," said the commissioner.

"I don't give a fuck!" cried Baron Jules as he was hustled towards the door. "I'll be back. I'll be back to piss all over the place." He broke into laughter. The commissioner and the servants threw him down the front steps. He rolled into the gutter. "I don't give a fuck," he cried once more. "You're all done for."

7

AFTER the eviction of Baron Jules the cocktail party at Lorque's house soon came to an end. Back in her studio apartment, after making herself a cup of tea and taking a bath, Aimée stood in front of the bathroom sink and, looking at her reflection in the mirror, spoke to herself:

"Well, it's the same as ever, isn't it? It seems slow, but actually it is quite fast. Sex always comes up first. Then money questions. And then, last, come the old crimes. You have seen other towns, my sweet, and you'll see others, knock on wood." She tapped her head. In the mirror, poorly illuminated by the fluorescent lighting built into the bathroom cabinet, her white reflection likewise tapped its head without smiling. "Come on, my sweet," she repeated, "the crimes come last, and you have to be patient."

She drank her tea and went to bed and slept soundly.

8

OVER THE next three weeks Aimée got into a routine. Accompanied by Maître Lindquist, she viewed several properties that were for sale in Bléville and the surrounding area. Each time she wavered, but was so charming that the realtor could not hold her rejections against her; on the contrary, he was more and more willing to humor her every whim.

Aimée's life was well ordered and well filled. She took tea in the morning, lunched on grilled meat at the Grand Café de l'Anglais, and had eggs or soup for dinner. The moment seemed far off when she would once more crave a choucroute. (Her weight had dropped to forty-five kilos. It was always like that when she was focused.) In the daytime she mingled with the local elite and made connections. Twice a week she went horseback riding at a country club, three times a week she played tennis. She also golfed, and on Friday nights she went to the casino, where she gambled very little. Twice a week, too, she honed her martial-arts skills at the Jules Ferry Center, a place where the elite were never to be seen. (She familiarized herself with the *nunchaku*, a weapon hitherto unknown to her.) And she became well known to the well-to-do of Bléville, and they to her. She observed their manners and customs, and especially the tensions and passions that existed amongst them; she observed them ceaselessly, attentively, patiently.

In the evenings, in her studio apartment, she made notes or added to earlier ones on record cards of some kind. She wrote with a small green fountain pen with a gold nib, using violet ink, and she moved her lips as she wrote.

Returning after a game of bridge or a long conversation with the voluble Christiane Moutet, she would write such things as: *Sonia Lorque had a foul life before she met Lorque. Mixture of gratitude and love. A solid couple, more solid than either thinks.* Or else she might write: *They say that L and L controls the construction business Géraud and Sons, which built the fish market. No competitive bids invited.*

When she finished writing, she would reread her notes several times before tidying them away in one of the drawers of the chest.

During the third week after Aimée's arrival in Bléville, the young woman left town briefly. She took the train one evening, arrived in Paris before midnight, changed stations by taxi, and caught another train. She had her slim attaché case and a large Delsey vanity case she had bought in Bléville. She had not reserved a seat on the train, but there were few travelers at that time of year, and she easily managed to find a comfortable spot.

About five thirty in the morning her train stopped for three minutes in a small town in the center of France. Aimée got off, walked out of the long gray railway station, crossed the Place de la Gare, and awoke the night man at the Grand Hôtel du Commerce et des Étrangers. At this time she was wearing a flowered dress beneath her coat and an opulent auburn wig. She took a room, awaking automatically at eight thirty as she had intended. She had rather good command of her body. At an earlier stage of her life she had been alienated from it in many ways. In particular, she could not get to sleep without a strong dose of barbiturates, nor wake up properly without a strong dose of stimulants, nor for that matter put up with her husband and the rest of her existence without quantities of appetite suppressants and tranquilizers, not to mention glasses of wine. But these days all that had changed. Aimée had control over her body; she had fallen asleep instantly and she woke up at the time of her choosing.

She showered, put her wig back on, and picked up the room phone. Croissants and hot chocolate were brought up to her. She ate heartily. Her demeanor had changed. A little later, smoking a menthol cigarette, she telephoned her financial adviser.

"Madame Souabe, what a marvelous surprise!" cried Maître Queuille when they met at the hotel for an aperitif and dinner together. "You haven't changed at all, how wonderful!"

"Nor have you, Roland," replied Aimée.

They talked business. They examined operating accounts and extracts from the land registry. Aimée gave the accountant sixty thousand francs that she had brought with her.

"Always cash! Highly suspect, I must say," joked Maître Queuille without malice.

He wrote out a receipt. He remarked that his sister had spent the month of September in England with her husband. The couple had not, however, been lucky enough to see Aimée on British television. The adviser asked Aimée, whom he continued to address as Madame Souabe, whether she had any thoughts of returning to France and finding work here. Aimée answered that she had grown accustomed to living and working in England.

"Well, of course," said Maître Queuille. He only half believed that this young woman was an actress in Great Britain, as she claimed, and he was even less convinced that she appeared in television commercials. Maître Queuille had a lively, prurient imagination. He rather suspected that his client was in fact a call girl.

A while later Aimée and the adviser exchanged smiles and parted company. Aimée ran a few errands, then boarded a Chausson country bus. During the eighteen-kilometer ride, she browsed through a local newspaper. For quite some time now she had stopped buying the Paris papers. But in this local sheet she suddenly came upon the information she had searched for in vain in the national press two or three weeks earlier. DEADLY HUNTING read the headline of a short piece on a bloody accident in which the father of a family was killed and his two sons wounded. *This*, concluded the article, *brings to a total of six the number of victims of hunting accidents since the beginning of the month. On the 2nd, M. Morin and M. Cardan shot each other in the vicinity of Saint-Bonnet-Tronçais (Allier). Two days later came the sad news from eastern France that M. François Roucart, a stock breeder, had been killed by a hunter not only inept but as yet unidentified. Are we heading for a time when hunting is more lethal to humans than to game? It is a fair question.*

Aimée kept the paper when she got off the coach in a village of two or three hundred souls. She walked through the village and started up a rock-strewn path angling up a hillside. The sky was gray and stormy. Aimée covered some four or five hundred meters. She kept wrenching her ankles on the rocks. She was sweating, even though the temperature was no more than eight or nine degrees above freezing and she was hardly well bundled up.

She entered a hamlet at the edge of a wood of oak and beech. Pushing open a small metal door she came into the sandy courtyard of a stone house. Lichen and moss covered the walls. The doorway to the house was open. Aimée stood on the threshold and looked around the main room with its dark-purple tiled floor. In the half darkness she could make out a stove, a heavy table covered with an oilcloth, and a large bed piled high with eiderdowns and adorned with shiny copper fittings. A plate, a glass, silverware, and a saucepan were drying by the sink on a draining board of blackish stone.

Aimée turned around. From the doorway she looked down over the vegetable garden that sloped away from the house beyond the sandy courtyard. Down in the valley the village could be seen beneath the gray sky, and fat white cows grazed in garishly green fields. Truck farms bordered a river. In the middle of the vegetable garden sat a woman in a straw hat, her back to the house. Aimée went down the three front steps and approached her.

"Mama?"

The woman did not react. Aimée went around the chair and stood in front of her. The mother started, then closed her mouth and pursed her lips. She was a woman of about sixty, frail, with white hair pulled back and a pale puffy face with heavy eyelids. Her eyes narrowed. She was wearing a black cotton apron quadrilled by faint white pinstripes, a black woolen shawl, slate-gray cotton socks rumpled up at her ankles, and men's black shoes. She had positioned herself between a row of potatoes and a lettuce patch.

"Don't you have your hearing aid?" asked Aimée, articulating slowly so that the woman could lip-read the syllables; and when no reply, no reaction was forthcoming, she shouted, "Where is your gizmo, for God's sake?"

"I don't know," answered the mother. "Don't swear. So you came to pay me a visit. You scared me."

"I came by to settle some things up," said Aimée, calmer now. "I've told Maître Queuille to increase your monthly payment. You shouldn't stay here alone ... you should get someone to be with you. I've told you before."

"Yes," said the mother.

Aimée delved in her bag.

"I brought you some tobacco and a present."

She handed the mother some packages of shag and a parcel tied with a ribbon. The mother slowly unwrapped the parcel and extracted a mauve cotton blouse with a motif of tiny white flowers. She held it up before her with both hands, shaking it slightly to unfold it. Then she refolded it distractedly, put it on her knees, and placed her hands over it.

"It's very pretty," she said, staring down into the valley.

Aimée nibbled at the side of her thumb without realizing it. She went back around the chair and stood still for a moment behind her mother's back.

"You bitch!" she said. "I hate you. God, I wish you would die!"

"Are you doing all right?" asked the mother. "What about your job? Your husband?"

She did not turn to see whether Aimée replied.

"In a little while," she went on, "the Father will be coming over. I'll make coffee. You could stay if you like and drink coffee with us."

"I have to leave," said Aimée.

She turned away and headed for the sandy courtyard and the little metal door.

"But," said the mother, "perhaps you have to leave."

Aimée reached Paris just as day was breaking. With time to kill before the Bléville train departed, she went for a walk. Near the Place du Châtelet, she was accosted by a broad-shouldered man in a chiné overcoat; his wavy hair glistened with hairspray. He followed her for a while. She accepted a light from him.

"Wouldn't you like to have a drink somewhere?" asked the man. "We can go to my place."

With her cigarette between her fingers, Aimée threw her head back and laughed.

"Why, you little devil!" said the man, quite pleased.

He grabbed Aimée's wrist with one hand, her waist with the other, and tried to kiss her on the neck. Aimée pulled away and took a step backwards, then swiftly came forward again and slapped the man. He reddened and reciprocated.

"So that's it, you filthy lesbo!" he cried.

For a few moments the two kept on slapping each other across the face. Then Aimée grew calm. Taking a very rapid half step back, she struck the man just under the nose with the side of her hand. He reeled back, staggered, and fell to the ground on his rear. He was pressing both hands to his snout.

"Oo! Oo!" he kept crying. "Ouch! Ouch! Ouch!"

His eyes were filling with tears. Aimée walked away.

In the Rue de Rivoli she took a taxi, retrieved her bags from the left-luggage office, and changed stations. There were still two long hours to wait before her train left, and she spent them in a brasserie. Then at last she was on her way back to Bléville.

9

ON THE day of her return, Aimée slept for a good many hours. Eventually she picked up the newspaper she had bought the day before, cut out the article concerning the death of Roucart, and filed it along with other clippings referring to other deaths: a factory owner in Bordeaux, five months earlier, asphyxiated on account of a faulty heater; a Parisian doctor drowned at La Baule in the early summer; and several more. Aimée used the remainder of the newspaper to line the kitchen trash can. That evening she ate no dinner. Using a little machine, she made copies of twenty or so keys that she had taken from the Bléville station luggage lockers. This was the second time she had copied keys in Bléville. By the time she finished, around ten o'clock, she had duplicates of keys to all the station's self-service luggage lockers.

"One of your neighbors has complained, Madame," said the girl at the reception desk the next morning as she was leaving. "Last night late, there was an electrical sound coming from your room."

"An electrical sound? Ah, yes," replied Aimée. "My hair dryer. It won't happen again."

"I am so glad you were able to come," said Lindquist later that day, in midafternoon. "But this is nothing really special. Just wait till summer, when I get you acquainted with our village festivals!"

Aimée nodded her head as though intrigued. Unusually, it was sunny and dry. The sea air was fresh and bracing, but people were well wrapped up, wearing scarves. In front of a main house two long tables with white tablecloths had been set up and laden with masses of hors d'oeuvres, cold cuts, and pastries, as well as a good many corked liter bottles of cider. The guests strolled on pastureland planted with apple trees. Variegated cattle could be seen in the distance. Once again Bléville's elite were assembled. The occasion was the baptism of a new addition to a filthy-rich family of graziers. Aimée had not been invited, but Lindquist had taken it upon himself to bring her.

"There is an especially beguiling game they play," the realtor was saying. "Young girls from the region, pretty ones preferably, are put in a paddock and blindfolded. Then a greased piglet is released among them. The girls are supposed to catch it if they can. But of course it's very hard with the slippery animal. The little pig squeals, and the little girls squeal too. It's quite captivating."

"I'm sure it is."

"And speaking of piglets," Lindquist exclaimed, "just look at that one!" He pointed to a six- or eight-month-old mite in a country-woman's lap.

The woman was forcing baby food into the mouth of the red-faced tot. The tot was shrieking at the top of its lungs and struggling. Suddenly it burped loudly and threw up everything it had swallowed.

"You disgusting little brat!" cried the woman furiously.

"Not to mention the egg-and-spoon race," Lindquist was saying now. "And the belote tournaments! For sheer entertainment you can't beat it!"

"I can hardly wait, dear Maître Lindquist," replied Aimée, who was watching Sinistrat and Mme Lenverguez slipping away towards the barns on the far side of the crowd.

By this time the baby was dead, though its mother had not yet noticed the fact. Mme Lenverguez and Sinistrat disappeared. Lindquist and Aimée went on chatting for a few minutes, bumping into and greeting the Tobies, the Moutets, and various other guests. Sinistrat's wife was sitting on a chair with her back to the wall of the main house and rubbing her ear morosely. All of a sudden, from the middle of the pasture, the countrywoman whose baby had vomited set up a mad, endless wailing and began beating herself about the head with her fists.

A great deal of commotion and shouting ensued. Some people crowded around the dead baby and the wailing mother. Others drew away as quickly as they could, vociferating, falling over their feet, waving their arms, and shaking their heads. Cries for help went up: "Sinistrat!" "Doctor!" After a moment Sinistrat arrived from the direction of the barns and pushed his way through the people. Aimée noticed that he had misbuttoned his fly. He undid the clothing of the tiny corpse, sounded the chest, and attempted mouth-to-mouth resuscitation, but he could not revive the child.

"He's dead," declared Sinistrat.

The mother's cries redoubled. She had to be pacified. All the groups of guests had broken up. People were banging into one another. Between two shoulders Aimée caught a brief glimpse of the dead baby's red face. She immediately experienced a violent stomach cramp and her teeth began to chatter.

"I want—I want to leave," she said to Lindquist.

The realtor looked at her impatiently, not understanding and making no reply. Aimée walked around him and crossed the orchard on the diagonal. She ran into Sonia Lorque, who tried to take her arm. Aimée stamped her foot on the grass, pulled free of the blonde-haired woman, and hastened towards the end of the paddock. The cries of the mother had ceased after an injection from Sinistrat. Behind the tables with their tablecloths and unopened bottles, women in gaily colored clothes were all weeping. As she went through the open gate, Aimée was striding firmly, almost running.

She covered a kilometer before fully collecting herself. She was still trembling a little. She looked out for a roadside distance marker. The sky was clouding over. After a while she found what she was seeking: a stone marked BLÉVILLE 3.5 KM. She kept on walking, rubbing her arms. She was wearing a flower-patterned silk dress that came down to just below the knee and a white wool jacket with her shoulder bag slung across her chest. It began to rain, just a little at first but then heavily. In a few minutes the young woman was soaked and her curls all gone. An ancient black Renault 4CV came along, its wings dented and dappled with dull orange paint. The car braked, and water sprayed across the crumbling roadway. At the wheel was Baron Jules. He opened the door and signaled to Aimée to come over. She did so without thinking about it. The man got out of the 4CV and went around to open the front passenger door. He held it open as Aimée stood immobile.

"I won't eat you," said the baron.

Aimée got into the car. In the confined interior she was obliged to pull her knees up high, exposing them. She pulled at her dress to cover them once more. Baron Jules was back behind the wheel. The 4CV set off again.

"The baby died," said Aimée.

"What's that you say?"

"A baby died. Not the one being baptized. Another baby. Belonging to a peasant woman. He vomited and then died."

"Calm yourself," said Baron Jules. "Take deep breaths."

He speeded up while on the highway, then slowed and turned into a narrow, graveled minor road running straight across fields of stubble. The suspension of the 4CV was very poor and its wiper blades very worn. Through the rain clusters of trees and an oddly spiral church steeple could be vaguely discerned. They reached a hamlet. Baron Jules braked and drove the 4CV through a white double gate, which was open, and down a broad drive. The white-wash on the gate was flaking badly. Beyond lay a very large garden and a kind of manor, a tiny manor burdened down with Lilliputian pepper-pot and pinnacle turrets. The garden had once been in the French manner but had clearly not been kept up for many years. With a squealing of tires on gravel, the 4CV drew up before a double staircase flanked by a pebble-dash balustrade.

"I want to go home," said Aimée. She shook herself. "I don't feel well. Take me back into town."

"You've had a shock," said Baron Jules. "You need to drink something. You need to dry off. You'll catch your death of cold."

The man got out of the car and went up the steps. Aimée got out too and followed him. They passed through a dim hall and entered a vast, very cluttered room with bow windows giving onto both the front and the rear of the residence.

"I have some calvados, and I must have the rest of a bottle of fairly decent scotch," said the baron. "And perhaps you would like some tea?" Aimée nodded. "I'll make tea. And let me find some towels so you can rub yourself down."

The man left through a small white door. Aimée took a few hesitant steps in the enormous room, which must have measured at least sixty or eighty square meters. It was crowded with sideboards, tables, cupboards, seats, sofas, knickknacks, and large cardboard boxes bearing such legends as BLACK AND WHITE and HÉNAFF LUNCHEON MEAT—JACK TAR'S TREAT. The pale paint on the walls and the plaster on the ceiling were all scaling off. The ceiling bore dirty brown circles above the shaded lamps. The furniture was thick with dust, and old breadcrumbs lay on the filth-ingrained Persian carpets. The baron returned carrying a tray laden with glasses and bottles. Slung over one shoulder was a hand towel with the logo of the SNCF, the French National Railways. He set the tray down and tendered the towel to Aimée. As the young woman rubbed her head he poured spirits from a crystal decanter into glasses bearing Mobil and Martini logos.

"When I break this decanter of mine," he said, "I'll replace it with one with advertising on it." He held out one of the glasses to Aimée, who reached for it with one hand as she continued toweling her hair with the other. "I am very interested in promotional items and free gifts," continued the baron. "Also in trash. I have no income, you see, and a man with no income is bound to take a great interest in free gifts and trash." He took a sip of brandy and clicked his tongue appreciatively. "Given the present state of the world, don't you know, with the increase of constant capital as compared with variable capital, a whole stratum of the poor is bound to be unemployed and live off free gifts and trash, and occasionally off various government subsidies. Do you know what I am saying?"

"I am not sure," said Aimée.

"Nor am I," said the baron. "But excuse me, please, I hear the kettle whistling."

He went off again through the small white door, leaving it open behind him.

"I'm glad I picked you up on the road," he shouted from the kitchen. "I wanted to see you again. I think you are mysterious. Are you mysterious?"

Aimée made no reply. The baron reappeared with another tray holding tea and cups.

"Alas, I have neither milk nor sugar at present," he said. "I must apologize for the condition in which I first appeared before you, I mean to say with my prick in my hand. It is I who must seem mysterious to you."

"Not really," said Aimée. "No big deal."

They drank their tea and glared at each other in silence, standing very close, with their noses in their cups.

"I am not mysterious," declared the baron at last. "I am an astronomer. Come, let me show you."

He went ahead of Aimée through the small white door and led her up a narrow staircase. They came to the second floor. Aimée, who had not finished her drink, an excellent calvados, was holding her glass. As they went down a passageway, the baron pointed into a bare room with a camp bed and covers, a naked bulb dangling from the ceiling, and cases of whiskey and cartons of cigarettes piled up against the walls.

"My bedroom," he said. "I'm not going to invite you in there to copulate; we are not well enough acquainted for that." And he continued on down the passageway. Here too there were boxes of spirits and cartons of cigarettes. "Would you like a few cartons of English cigarettes?" he asked. "I have various dealings with the Bléville seamen."

"No, thank you," replied Aimée.

"And I win stuff off them at cards," added the baron as he started up a very narrow spiral staircase at the end of the corridor. "I'm a very good player. And, frankly, they let me cheat. Because I make them laugh."

The spiral staircase led up an angle tower. Through leaded windows of colored glass Aimée looked down over the rear of the garden, where rabbits were running in and out of rain-soaked hutches. Then they came into a circular room directly beneath the tower's roof.

"Didn't I tell you I was an astronomer?" the baron cried triumphantly. Although they had climbed the staircase quickly, he was not out of breath. Nor was Aimée.

There were apertures in the roof, mirrors, a variety of glasses and telescopes, and, strewn on rolling enameled tables reminiscent of those used in hospitals, papers covered with notations in very tiny but very legible handwriting. So far as Aimée could tell, these were calculations and vaguely poetic thoughts on celestial bodies. Through a stained-glass window the blue-tinged rooftops of Bléville could be seen several kilometers away.

"It's a fine pastime, astronomy," said the baron, as he adjusted a telescope mounted at an almost vertical angle and pointing at an opening in the roof, a kind of skylight. "It's a fine pastime that harms no one and corresponds to my social rank and tastes. I love to observe." He looked at Aimée, who did not respond. He turned away and abruptly slapped the telescope down into a horizontal position. "Not just the stars, though—fine gentlemen too!" he cried. "Bléville is also worth observing. Not with this instrument, of course. But through cracks in the walls, through the chinks in people themselves, through keyholes." The baron turned away from the stained-glass window. "I have been watching this town for dozens of years," he explained. "I know everything there is to know about it." His expression was now frozen, empty. Muscles pulled his lips taut against his teeth. "So just fight bravely on, most gracious masters of capital!...you shall be allowed to rule for a short time. You shall be allowed to dictate your laws, to bask in the rays of the majesty you have created, to spread your banquets in the halls of kings, and to take the beautiful princess to wife—but do not forget that 'Before the door stands the headsman!'"

"What are you talking about?" demanded Aimée.

A little later, a little calmer now, as the pair went back down into the hall (on a wall of which hung a Weatherby Regency under-and-over double-barrel shotgun), Baron Jules further informed Aimée that, although the movements of men are not analogous to the movements of the stars, it sometimes seemed to him that they were, this on account of the posture that he had adopted, or rather that he had been obliged to adopt. These strange remarks made Aimée a little nervous, and she wanted to get away from this place. It was not long before the baron drove her back to Bléville. Yet when he left in his banged-up old 4CV, Aimée was sorry.

10

ONE OR two minutes after alighting from Baron Jules's 4CV in front of the Seagull Apartments, Aimée was opening the door of her studio when she heard a kind of strangled groan which made her shudder. Standing before her half-open door, she quickly turned her head. Some way down the corridor, another door was ajar. In the opening a little old lady could be seen. Aimée shook her head in irritation. Twice or three times a week she had noticed the old lady spying on her as she passed. She was an especially repulsive old woman by Aimée's lights, with her pendulous cheeks caked with white face powder and her purplish lipstick. This time, though, she seemed to be trying to address the young woman. Clutching the doorframe with one hand, she cleared her throat in a disgusting way. Aimée opened the door to her studio wide, went in, and slammed it behind her.

She put her bag down on a chair and went over to hang her woolen jacket in the armoire. Rustling sounds came from down the corridor, and then from right outside her apartment; a scratching noise seemed to emanate from the crack beneath the door, followed by snorts, a belch, and a cough. Aimée went back to the door and opened it in exasperation.

"What the hell do you want?" she demanded.

Only then did she see the old woman, silent now, lying on her stomach just outside her door, her face in a pool of vomit. Aimée grimaced in disgust. After a moment of hesitation, she went down on one knee and felt for the little old lady's pulse. She found none. With the tip of a fingernail she pulled back one of the woman's eyelids in search of some retinal reflex. Then she stood up, and, leaving the door open, went and picked up the telephone receiver and made an emergency call. Six or seven minutes later a police car and an ambulance pulled up in front of the building. Shortly thereafter, Police Commissioner Fellouque's personal car also drew up. A bald-headed doctor of about fifty, whom Aimée did not know, examined the old woman. She was dead. They took her away on a stretcher.

"She must have dragged herself along to your room to ask for help," said Commissioner Fellouque. Tall and dark, with a light mustache and dazzling white teeth, Fellouque was the cop whom Aimée had seen tossing Baron Jules out of Lorque's house. The young woman now poured him a cup of tea that she had just made. "Then," he went on, "she turned around intending to go back to her room and phone. Which is what she should have done in the first place. I doubt it would have made much difference though."

"Commissioner, is something unusual going on?" asked Aimée.

"What do you mean? What do you mean, something unusual?"

"Well, you are the commissioner, and you have taken the trouble to come out here," said Aimée. "The emergency services could have handled this. But perhaps . . ." She hesitated. "I saw a baby die in the same kind of way early this afternoon."

The commissioner rose from the bed, where he had sat down without being invited. He began gesturing with both arms and hunched his head back into his shoulders.

"I don't want people going crazy and spreading wild rumors!" he cried. "There's some kind of food poisoning going around, that's all." He dropped his arms and suddenly seemed calm and disdainful. "I have another dead person on my hands, the third, and there are a dozen or so people in the hospital, if you must know. I want no panic. You're not going to get on the phone, I hope?"

"The phone?"

"Yes, yes," said the commissioner. "You know how you women are amongst yourselves."

Aimée and the policeman looked wordlessly at each other for a moment. Fellouque seemed suspicious and exasperated. Aimée's attitude was contemptuous.

"Do you have any canned goods here?" asked the commissioner. The door to the studio, which had been pushed shut, was now opened wide by someone who was simultaneously knocking on it. "Ah, not you!" cried the commissioner. "Get the hell out of here! Leave us be!"

"This is a private residence," observed the intruder, a small man in his fifties with blue eyes and iron-gray hair as spiky as a bird's nest. He was wearing a long, beat-up leather jacket. "You have no right to kick me out, Fellouque," he added, turning to Aimée. "Press, my dear little lady. DiBona, *Dépêche de Bléville*. Might I speak with you?"

"You can not! You can not!" said Commissioner Fellouque, attempting to bar the fifty-year-old's way as he moved smiling towards Aimée.

"Lorque and Lenverguez are busy poisoning half the town, my dear madame," said DiBona. "We have cattle dying too. I must appeal to your public spirit. Don't tell me you are going to let this cop cover it all up?"

"It's not about covering anything up!" exclaimed Fellouque. "Malice is leading you astray, DiBona. You are raving." He turned to Aimée. "He is raving!"

"He wants to cover it up!" insisted DiBona.

"People are waiting for me to play bridge, gentlemen," said Aimée. "You must excuse me."

It took her a few minutes to get rid of the two men, but eventually Aimée found herself on her bicycle in the streets of Bléville. Her appointment was at five o'clock at the Moutets, for tea and a rubber of bridge with the couple and Sonia Lorque. She was not quite sure, in point of fact, considering the baby's death and the other alarms, that the game would take place. But she smiled as she pedaled. She liked crises.

In the end they did play bridge.

"We are completely shattered by this business," said the voluptuous Christiane Moutet, and indeed she seemed somewhat worried and overwrought. (Her husband was on the telephone in his study down the hallway, and his anxious and disgruntled exclamations could be heard.)

Sonia Lorque arrived one or two minutes after Aimée. The factory owner's wife also seemed tense and worried. But she was strikingly well turned out. Her eyebrows had been plucked recently, possibly that very afternoon. Her makeup had been applied with the greatest care, as though she had purposely sought to dazzle at this particular moment.

At first everyone agreed that it would be unthinkable to play a game of cards as if everything was normal after the ghastly event of the early afternoon.

"At least we can have a drink," said senior manager Moutet, who had finished his phoning. He wore a worried, slightly stupid expression. He nibbled at his reddish mustache.

They had drinks in the living room. The Moutets occupied a five-room apartment in the old town, completely refurbished. There was modern furniture, wall-to-wall carpeting, and reproductions of abstract paintings.

Since everyone was present, and no one knew what to say, the voluptuous Christiane Moutet ended up suggesting that after all they might play a little bridge. And play they did. But their hearts were not in it. Players were continually making remarks or engaging in chatter quite unrelated to the cards.

"One no trumps."

"No bid."

"No bid."

"Two spades," said Aimée.

"DiBona is an ass," said Sonia Lorque when Aimée told her about the reporter bursting into her studio earlier. "He takes himself for an American-style tabloid journalist," the blond woman went on. "Always unearthing scandals that don't exist."

"But this time," said Christiane Moutet in a soft voice, her eyes fixed on her cards, "there have been three deaths. A strange mixture of deaths: cows, babies, adults." She looked up. "This is really screwed up!" she cried. "Does nobody have any conception of what has happened?"

"Damn it! Damn it! They are looking into it!" said senior manager Moutet. "Are we here to play cards or to talk drivel?"

The telephone rang in his study. He got up from the table with a groan of disgust.

"Damn!" he said again.

He went into his study without closing the door. The women waited. They heard him saying hello, then shouting.

"What?"

Sonia Lorque brought her hand to her face. Her features passed through a series of changes that Aimée could not interpret but that she observed with curiosity. Down the hallway, senior manager Moutet went over to pull his office door closed. He could still be heard in an altercation with his interlocutor, though the details of the conversation were not discernible. Christiane Moutet lit a cigarette. Everyone pretended to be studying their hands or gazed at the green baize of the card table. With eyelids lowered, Aimée paid closer and closer attention to Sonia Lorque. The blonde covered her face with both hands when Moutet emerged from his study and came back into the living room. The man seemed beside himself.

"The bastard!" he cried. "Fucking hell!" The women stared at him. Sonia Lorque kept her hands over her face, but peeked at Moutet between her fingers. Moutet slumped into an armchair, then sprang up again and returned to his place at the table. He hunched forward. As he planted his elbows on the green felt his cards were swept off the table and fell to the floor. At the same moment Sonia Lorque rose and moved away from her chair, turning her back on the table. She did not make for a door, but instead toward a corner of the living room nowhere near an exit. Christiane Moutet gazed at her husband in alarm. Aimée watched Sonia Lorque with curiosity.

"The bastard!" said the senior manager again. "It's in my contract! And he thinks I'm going to take this lying down?"

"What are you saying?" demanded Christiane Moutet. "What's going on?"

"What's going on is I'm responsible for the cold-storage rooms. It's in my contract." Moutet spoke in slow tones. He seemed concerned to articulate clearly. "SON OF A BITCH! THIS IS UNBELIEVABLE! IMPOSSIBLE! CRAZY!"

"But what's going on?" Christiane Moutet asked again, very calmly, eyebrows barely raised.

Wheeling around, Sonia grabbed Christiane Moutet's wrist very roughly, startling her. Aimée kept watching.

"The cold rooms in the new fish market have been breaking down," said the blonde, speaking very fast. "That's what's going on. All three processing plants were working for three hours with rotten fish. And your husband is getting the blame for it."

"You must be joking," said Christiane Moutet.

"No."

Christiane Moutet stared at the blonde reflectively.

"No," repeated Sonia. "I heard my husband and Lenverguez talking. They were talking for an hour. It's your hubby who's going to be the fall guy."

"You little bitch!" said Christiane Moutet in a placid tone of voice. "You already knew about it. Bitch!" she said again, sounding surprised.

"Listen," said Sonia Lorque. "I am in a position to propose an arrangement."

Christiane Moutet rose. She delivered a resounding slap across the cheek to Sonia, which must have been audible ten meters away. Then she spat in her face. She careened into the bridge table, overturning it. The cards scattered. Aimée, sitting, drew on her cigarette. Sonia Lorque headed for the door. The side of her face was scarlet. Her makeup was running.

"Go ahead," said Christiane Moutet. "Piss off. Run and find your pantywaist of a husband."

"Too bad for you, sweetie," said Sonia.

"It's in my contract," repeated Moutet, still sitting motionless at his seat, hunched over, looking defeated and distraught. "I'm responsible. I'm screwed."

Sonia Lorque left the apartment, slamming the door behind her.

"Was I dreaming," Christiane asked Aimée, "or did that bitch talk about an arrangement?"

"About money," answered Aimée.

"What?"

"Someone has to go down," explained Aimée, "and they picked him. But they want to do it nice and quietly. They'll pay money for your guy to take everything on the chin without complaint."

"What do you know about it?" Suspicion flared suddenly in the brunette's eyes.

"It stands to reason, that's all," said Aimée.

Christiane Moutet looked at her blankly, even stupidly. She seemed to be finding it hard to focus on her own thoughts. Then she nodded and a little smile touched the edge of her mouth. Suddenly her face contorted with fury, as though the truth had just dawned on her.

"Without complaint!" she repeated. "Not a chance! We'll drag them through the mud, that's what we'll do!"

"Yes," said Aimée. "You should do that. If they are offering a deal, it means they have things to hide. You should stir the shit, all the shit you can." Aimée took two steps forward and used both hands to grab the brunette by the shoulders. "I'll help you," she said quickly. "I can dig stuff up."

"Stuff?"

"The dirt. I'll call you." Aimée let go of Christiane, turned on her heel, and for a moment stood facing senior manager Moutet, who was still sitting in his chair, shattered.

"Don't worry about it," she told him, and walked out the door, left the building, and almost crashed into Sonia Lorque on the sidewalk.

"How are they taking it?" Sonia wanted to know.

Aimée shrugged. She reached down to unlock the heavy motorcycle antitheft device fitted to her Raleigh. "Badly," she said. And, straightening up, she added, "They're going to fight."

"I am not involved in all this," said Sonia. "I am merely trying—"
She broke off. "No one can stop me from sticking with my husband."

"Of course, of course. Good for you. Bravo," said Aimée as she
straddled her bicycle. "You can all stick with your husbands. Stupid
cows."

She rode away on the Raleigh, pedaling vigorously. Whichever
way you go, there is a big hill to climb before you get out of Bléville.
Aimée headed east, inland. She climbed the entire hillside standing.
By the time she reached the top of the hill, she was panting, her forehead was running with sweat, and her armpits smelled rank. Sitting
back down on the saddle, she raced along the even road. Her teeth
were bared; she was excited. In a few minutes she reached the hamlet
where Baron Jules lived. The baron invited her in. He was wearing
blue jeans and a check cotton shirt frayed and fluffy at the collar and
cuffs, along with a velvet jacket. Aimée told him what had been happening. She described the scene at the Moutets. The baron asked her
why she had come straight to him to retail all this.

"I thought it would amuse you," she answered.

"You certainly thought no such thing!" scolded the baron with
irritation. The approach of nightfall made it very dark in the cluttered living room. The nobleman switched on a lamp with a shade
and stared suspiciously at Aimée, who had sat down in an armchair
with broken springs. "Think how long I have been observing those
people, my God! I have been observing them for thirty years and
more, it must be nearly forty now, yes indeed! Well, in all that time
they have not given me a single moment's amusement. They make
me want to vomit and destroy them."

"Yes," said Aimée, "precisely. But I'll believe it when I see it." She
shook her head violently, as though to get her thoughts straight or
shake off an unpleasant memory. She had the blank look of someone
suddenly unable to see the necessity of what they have decided to do.
But she quickly collected herself. "Yes, yes, yes, precisely," she repeated, nodding and leaning forward excitedly. "Moutet is going to
fight this. He needs weapons to do it—and allies. I daresay someone
like Dr. Sinistrat will line up with him. And then there's this guy

DiBona, from the *Dépêche de Bléville*, I think—yes, that's it. If they dig up stuff against Lorque and Lenverguez, there'll be havoc."

"Why should I give a shit?" demanded Baron Jules.

"The dirt—you've got to have it, considering all the time you've been observing Bléville," said Aimée. "If you really want to vomit and destroy them, this is your moment."

The baron gazed at her for a moment, then burst out laughing. His laugh was painful to him. It literally doubled him up.

"You're insane," he said, with tears in his eyes.

"I've said what I had to say," replied Aimée tranquilly. She got out of the armchair with the broken springs and made for the door with her hands thrust into her pockets.

"Wait!" cried the baron, plunging after her. "You are a terrifyingly negative and beautiful person." He tripped over one of the filthy rugs and fell to one knee. "Listen up!" he said. "Just what is your interest in all this?"

Aimée was already through the hall and out the front door. She ran down the steps, mounted her bicycle, and set the dynamo for light, for night had fallen. Puffing, the baron emerged at the top of the darkened front steps. He was rubbing his knee.

"Wait, for God's sake!" he cried. "What is your interest in this, for God's sake? Don't leave. Explain!"

But Aimée, her tires creating a crackle and spray of gravel, was heading full-tilt for the gate, then she was through it and gone.

11

THAT SAME evening, as he returned home a few minutes before midnight, the journalist DiBona found Baron Jules waiting for him on the stairs of his apartment building. As DiBona told it the next day, he had the impression at the moment that the man was drunk, although you never really knew with the baron. What is certain is that the impecunious nobleman was highly excited and vexed. DiBona invited him into his apartment and they had a conversation. (At some point during their exchange, DiBona telephoned the *Dépêche*'s printshop; and later that night, after the conversation was over, he left his home once more and went to reset the entire front page of the next day's paper and made some changes to the inside pages.) As the two men were talking the baron drank a great deal of red wine that DiBona poured for him and repeatedly buried his face in his hands, pressing his palms hard against the area just below his eyes, then abruptly moving them downwards, still applying pressure, as though seeking to wipe away deep stains, or perhaps tattoos, from his cheeks. He was also continually rising from his chair and then sitting down again. He paced back and forth across the dull parquet floor. At times he was voluble, at others information had to be dragged out of him. Throughout the interview he displayed a quite remarkable animosity towards DiBona, for after all the baron had come of his own accord, no one had forced him and nothing obliged him to reveal things to the reporter or to talk to him as he chose to do.

For example, after evoking Bléville's past in a vague and abstract manner, and after DiBona asked him what was so special about that past, Baron Jules well-nigh shouted.

"Nothing! Nothing special at all! Corruption, influence peddling, swindles of every stripe, sexual turpitude—just like anywhere else. But do you want the wherewithal to destroy Lorque and Lenverguez, or don't you give a shit?"

"Don't get angry," said DiBona. He was setting up an enormous, dusty, ancient tape recorder on a round table covered with an oilcloth. "It wasn't me who brought you here," the journalist pointed out. "Anyway, we'll record what you have to say, in case it is of interest."

"Interest?" repeated the baron. "You little twerp, I tell you I know everything about this town. I know everything about you too, Di-Bona. I know what you did in 1943."

DiBona cast an inscrutable glance at the baron.

"If you don't mind," said the journalist, switching on his recorder, "let's stick to Lorque and Lenverguez . . ."

The next day, in a town already roiled by the furor over the rotten fish, the mood deteriorated even further, and quickly. THE TRUTH ON LORQUE AND LENVERGUEZ was the headline in the *Dépêche de Bléville*, while the subtitle read: "Deadly Canned Goods Just the Latest in a Long Series of Scandals." From that point on, the peace that usually reigned in Bléville was irremediably shattered, and things only got worse over the following days. Each morning the *Dépêche* gave the "Latest on the Scandals" and followed up by launching new bugaboos. Nothing earthshaking. It merely emerged, in a general way, that Bléville's municipal government and public treasury had always been in thrall to the interests of Lorque and Lenverguez. This was scant justification for outrage. But passions were aroused by the deaths of the baby and two or three old people, along with thirty or so cows, all poisoned by L and L products, by Old Sea-Pilot canned goods and Happy Baby baby food. Many solid citizens pretended to be appalled; quite a few, out of stupidity, really were appalled. Others stood up for Lorque and Lenverguez. The bourgeoisie of Bléville was split in two.

At noontime the atmosphere at the Grand Café de l'Anglais would be electric. As early as eleven thirty, DiBona, often joined by Georges Rougneux and Robert Tobie, the bookseller and the pharmacist, would lay claim to the back room of the brasserie. The men would drink Ricard, unfolding that day's *Dépêche*, passing its pages from hand to hand, commenting loudly and laughing maliciously. Around a quarter past twelve, senior manager Moutet would appear and be slapped on the back by the drinkers. Though not indicted as yet, he had twice been deposed by a magistrate. He spoke more quickly than formerly, and his voice seemed higher pitched. His complexion was more florid, as were his gestures, and each time he came he downed several full pints of German beer. A little later, between house calls, Sinistrat would become part of the noisy group for forty minutes. Affecting a smile steelier than usual and a curt tone, lowering his eyelids somewhat and throwing his head back to blow cigarette smoke towards the grubby ceiling, the doctor played the subtle analyst, the icy extremist, the Machiavelli.

"So old Lenverguez has two good reasons, doesn't he," DiBona asked him, "for not clasping you to his bosom? There's your articles, and then there's his wife ..."

Sinistrat smiled, making no effort to contest the insinuation. Then he suddenly put on a serious face.

"This has nothing to do with personal matters," he said. "Fundamentally, this is political."

At one o'clock precisely, Lorque and Lenverguez, along with their wives, would enter the brasserie, scan the room with a distant air, share a few friendly handshakes, and go upstairs to take lunch on the second-floor balcony. From the back room, their field of vision limited by the balcony which extended above their heads, DiBona and his allies were obliged, in order to inspect the factory owners' party, to peer over their glasses and beer mugs and hold up their chins, which gave them a weak and furtive look.

During these days Aimée made no appearance at the Grand Café de l'Anglais, nor anywhere in town, except for a daily trip from her studio to and from a tobacco shop on the harbor front, where she bought the papers and crime novels. The rest of the time she stayed in her apartment doing a little thinking and reading the papers and crime novels.

Early in the morning of the fourth day, she received a telephone call from Baron Jules, who had apparently gone to ground since his interview with DiBona. He sounded nervous, tired, filled, perhaps, by a kind of perverse glee—and bitter.

"Yes," Aimée told him. "Alright. But maybe you would rather come over here?" The baron said no. "Whenever you like then," replied Aimée. "Right away, if you wish." But the baron demurred, and said he would rather she came at exactly five o'clock. "That's fine," said Aimée.

She spent the day in her studio, reading, then watching a television show designed to edify housewives and an episode from a stupid and restful American series. At four o'clock she opened a can of corned beef and ate the contents. Then she went out. She went by the tobacco shop for the papers. The *Dépêche* had new revelations, accusing Maître Lindquist of corruption and calling for the opening of judicial investigations into Lorque and Lenverguez and the attorney-realtor. Aimée got on her Raleigh and rode to the baron's. He met her on the front steps.

"Could you stay for a while?" he asked immediately. "Till eight o'clock?"

"I don't know," replied Aimée.

The baron was wearing wide-striped pants and a blue seaman's sweater. He was sockless in disintegrating tennis shoes. He had not shaved that morning and tough white whiskers could be seen on his pink cheeks. His features were drawn and his reddened eyes had dark rings beneath them. He seemed unable to stand still. He took Aimée by the arm and led her haphazardly through the garden. It was a mild day. The sky was a low and uniform gray. From far-off fields of stubble came the throb of a tractor's engine.

"It's coming from me, everything they are putting out in the *Dépêche*," said the baron.

"Oh, I don't doubt it."

"You should be happy."

Aimée shrugged. "Yes."

"Well, I am not happy," said the baron.

"No?" Aimée shook her head.

"There's not one of them that can redeem the others," said the baron. "You really think DiBona deserves to be given ammunition? Do you know what he, DiBona, was doing in 1943?"

"I couldn't care less."

"He was turning in Allied parachutists to the Germans."

"I couldn't care less," Aimée repeated.

"You egged me on," said Baron Jules grumpily. "You pushed me into this. You got me to set one clique against the other. You got me entangled with them. I'm not happy about that."

"If you're not happy, you can go fuck yourself," Aimée suggested. "I'm cold."

The baron took Aimée's arm once more. By this time the pair had circled the residence. The baron led the young woman towards a small back door. They went in, climbed three steps, and emerged into the hall where the Weatherby Regency shotgun hung. The baron started up the stairs.

"Just wait," he said with venomous satisfaction. "You'll see."

Aimée followed him up the stairs and then up to the observatory. The stained-glass windows cast colored light on the walls, on the instruments, on the wheeled enameled table on which lay several brown kraft-paper envelopes.

"I've been thinking things over, these last three days," said the baron. "What I've revealed about these people amounts to nothing. I can do much better. On the others too I can do far better. I can decapitate this town."

"So go ahead," said Aimée in a bored voice.

Smiling, the baron tapped with the flat of his hand on the brown envelopes, which were bulging. Then he stood back and leaned against a wall with his arms crossed. Aimée picked up one of the envelopes. It was marked "Jacques Lorque." She glanced at a few more of them, marked "DiBona," "Dr. Claude Sinistrat," "Lindquist," and so on.

"They are not sealed. Take a look inside," said the baron. "Half of them are going to prison, and the rest will have no honor left. Go on, take a look."

"I'm not interested. I couldn't care less," said Aimée, sounding weary and bored, and she pushed the envelopes away.

"Vipers! Swine! Dogs!" cried Baron Jules in a high-pitched voice. He stepped away from the wall in excitement. "They're all crooks, can't you see that?"

"Crooks or not. Even if they were honest..." said Aimée. She did not finish her sentence.

"I have called them all here for six o'clock. I'm going to show them what's in the envelopes. These are all just copies. Wait till you see their faces."

"Do you plan to sell them the originals?"

"What do you take me for?" yelled the baron.

"Oh, I said that just to get your goat. What are you proposing to do?"

"I'm going to send all this stuff to the Paris papers," replied the baron. "But first I'm going to show them these copies, make them sweat with fear, so they know what's coming to them."

The baron took a few steps, shaking with silent laughter. At that moment the sun, shining through a stained-glass pane, threw a bright streak of scarlet across the baron's neck. The man looked as though his throat had been slashed. Aimée felt a certainty and an anxiety that made her wobble on her feet.

"Why are you pulling a face?" asked the baron. "Isn't this what you wanted? It *is* what you wanted!" he said with conviction. "I don't get it, but it is what you wanted."

Aimée wheeled, and tore off down the staircase. Stunned, the baron did not move for a moment. Then he raced down the stairs in pursuit.

"Don't deny it!" he cried. "I know you wanted this!"

"Leave me alone. Get away from me," said Aimée as she crossed the hall at top speed, passing the Weatherby Regency mounted on the wall.

She left the house, leaped onto her Raleigh. For a second time she rode off the property with the baron, now out on the front steps, calling vainly after her.

"They'll be here in twenty minutes," he shouted. "Stay! You'll see them go white about their ugly gills. Stay!"

Aimée disappeared. The baron let his arms drop to his sides. Thwarted and seeming unsure of himself, he went back inside. Meanwhile, Aimée sped along the road, left the hamlet behind, and headed towards Bléville. After a few hundred meters, she noticed a copse on the right. She braked and put a foot on the ground. Then, holding the bicycle by the handlebars, she left the road. There was no one in sight. She went into the clump of trees and hid there with her bike.

12

HIDDEN in the copse, Aimée did not have long to wait. After barely a quarter of an hour, she began to see cars going by on the road to the hamlet. The vehicles continued to pass for ten minutes or so, sometimes one or two minutes apart, sometimes closer. There were three cars separated by only fifty or sixty meters, apparently traveling in a group. Altogether, Aimée counted more than ten vehicles. Standing in the sheltered half darkness of the clump of trees, invisible amid the prickly branches, she recognized most of the drivers, among them the bookseller Rougneux at the wheel of a Renault 6, the pharmacist Tobie in a Citroën GS, Lorque with his brownish eyelids driving a large tobacco-colored Mercedes. A chauffeur in street clothes and a cap was at the wheel of another Mercedes with the skinny, laconic Lenverguez in the back. Dr. Sinistrat, attorney and realtor Lindquist, and senior manager Moutet in his Alfa Romeo also passed. Two or three other vehicles were driven by people unknown to Aimée, among them a Citroën 1200 Kg van with a sign on the side reading GÉRAUD AND SONS—BUILDERS—ENGINEERS—PUBLIC WORKS. The journalist DiBona brought up the rear at five past six, flying along on a mud-streaked Polish WSK motorcycle in a leather coat and an English crash helmet with a visor.

Then the landscape was empty once more as far as the eye could see. Standing still in the obscurity of the copse, Aimée smoked two cigarettes. She felt rather cold. She crouched by her bike, unscrewed the valve of the rear wheel, and pressed down. The tire deflated. Once it was flat, Aimée stood up again.

Once more the cars began to pass by, returning from the hamlet now and heading towards Bléville. They were traveling fast, the pitch of their engines changing as drivers shifted into a higher gear and left the houses behind. The roaring motors seemed to express anger and fear. Aimée let them all pass by without showing herself, all save Lorque's tobacco-colored Mercedes, which she watched out for, and which made its appearance a little after the others, bringing up the rear. When she saw it emerge from the hamlet, going at a reasonable speed, she came out of the trees and went back onto the road. Holding her bicycle by the handlebars, she positioned herself in the middle of the roadway. With one hand she signaled the car to stop.

"I have a flat," she said to Lorque, pointing to the deflated tire. "Could you take me back to town?"

Lorque helped her put the Raleigh in the roomy trunk of the Mercedes. He got back behind the wheel and Aimée sat beside him in the passenger seat. The man's lips were tight, his glance distracted. He started the car fairly gently, then accelerated.

"Don't go too fast," said Aimée. "I am not what I seem to be. I have a proposal for you, one that will surprise you. Between now and when we get to Bléville, you have to hear me out, and you have to answer me yes or no."

A few moments later, Lorque parked the Mercedes behind the fish market on a dirty deserted street because he and Aimée had not finished their discussion. Night had come. Cats ran among piles of empty shells. Inside the car, Lorque and Aimée talked and sat in silence by turns. At one point Lorque covered his face with both hands and it seemed as if Aimée had spoken sharply to him. At another moment he burst out laughing, but his laughter appeared to be bitter.

"You might be in cahoots with the baron," said Lorque at one juncture.

"That's a risk you must take."

"It is indeed a risk."

"My friends are also taking a risk," said Aimée.

"Do I know these friends of yours? Have I ever met them?"

Aimée shook her head. "You have never seen them. And you never will."

"I have to think this over for a few hours," said Lorque. "I'll telephone you tonight."

"On the phone," said Aimée, "just say yes or no. Three hours after your call, I'll meet you here. The problem will have been taken care of. I'll give you the documents that concern you. You will have deposited the forty thousand francs in the self-service locker. You will give me the key to the locker."

"It would be simpler if—"

"No discussion," ordered Aimée.

"It's a large sum," said Lorque. Aimée made no reply. She stared straight ahead through the windshield. Lorque shrugged. "Very well," he said, turning towards the young woman. "But I'll need some proof that the problem really has been taken care of. How am I to know—"

"A Polaroid print," said Aimée. "Would that do?"

"That will do."

Aimée consulted her watch. Seven ten. The guns and ammo stores would be closing soon. She turned a placid face to Lorque.

"Fine," she said, to end the conversation.

"I am flabbergasted," said Lorque, smiling almost despite himself. "I can't believe my ears, honestly. I had found you strange, but this . . . no. I'm still not quite sure it's real. I'm going to need an hour or two to decide whether it's real or not."

"It's real," said Aimée. "My proposal is real. Everything is perfectly real."

Lorque grabbed Aimée's wrist and looked intensely into her eyes. He was half sneering, despite himself. With his other hand he clasped the nape of her neck, pulling the young woman towards him and giving her a breathless kiss. She let herself be kissed. His mouth was warm. Then she pulled away.

"That's enough," she said.

"You excite me," said Lorque. "Are you going to disappear afterwards? Yes, of course you are. You should—" He broke off. "I could—" He broke off a second time, gesturing vaguely.

"No, out of the question," said Aimée as she opened the car door.

Lorque did not help her get the bicycle out of the trunk. As soon as she closed it, he started the engine and put his lights on. The Mercedes drew away silently and disappeared. Aimée got her pump and reinflated the rear tire. At about seven thirty she visited a hunting and fishing store in the center of Bléville. There she bought a supply of 12-gauge large-shot ammunition.

Thereafter, Aimée made calls on people in various parts of town and negotiated with them until late that night. As a rule, the young woman had found that she was obliged in the first instance to make her proposition to interlocutors in a guarded way, or else in a way that made it seem like a joke. But this time, in contrast with the way things had sometimes been in the past, in other towns, Aimée had an obvious way to broach her subject.

"I know," she told nearly all those she parlayed with, "that the baron possesses documents that you would like to retrieve. I have friends who are ready to retrieve them for you. No, don't interrupt, just listen."

The rest followed, more or less quickly, more or less easily.

"My dear Madame Joubert, you astound me!" exclaimed Lindquist, but then she spoke to him brutally, using malicious, coarse language that shattered the man's façade of respectability and left him speechless; and he offered little resistance when she made her proposition.

Aimée got back to the Seagull Apartments around eleven o'clock. She disturbed the manageress, who was watching television, and announced that she would be leaving Bléville that very night. The manageress hemmed and hawed a little, but since Aimée was paid up through the end of the week, there was not much she could say. The young woman went on up to her studio apartment and packed her bags. The telephone rang. She answered. Lorque was on the line.

"I still can't believe it," he said.

"Is it yes or no?" demanded Aimée.

"It's yes. What do I have to lose?"

"Fine," said Aimée.

She ended the conversation by depressing the cradle switch with her thumb, and without replacing the receiver called the telephone standard in front of the train station with its enamel plaque reading KEEP YOUR TOWN CLEAN! In response to Aimée's call a taxi appeared in front of the apartment around twelve fifteen. The young woman was already waiting in the lobby with her luggage. She had herself driven to the station. There she put her bags in the self-service lockers. She kept only her handbag, which among other things held a small Polaroid camera, doubles of every key to the lockers, and six 12-gauge shotgun cartridges. There was a 4:35 a.m. boat train that picked up connecting passengers arriving by sea, and she booked a ticket to Paris on it. Then she went back out of the station, took another taxi, and returned to the Seagull Apartments. Wheeling out her bicycle, she slung her bag over her shoulder and pedaled energetically to the baron's.

It was ten past one when she got there. Lorque had phoned to say yes just an hour and a half earlier. Aimée grimaced when she saw light coming from the baron's bedroom on the second floor of the house. Taking care not to let the gravel crunch underfoot, the young woman slipped through the shadows and leaned her bicycle against the wall of the manor. Perfectly still in the cold of the night, she waited without feeling anything. The light went out. Aimée waited for a good quarter of an hour longer. Her teeth chattered now and again, her stomach fluttered, and she was sweating, but she still felt nothing. At this point, she could have gone back to the station, opened all the lockers, taken whatever money was already deposited in them, and vanished on the 4:35 train. She rooted in her bag. She worked her hands slowly into a pair of latex gloves. She walked around the house. Disturbed, the rabbits made muted sounds as they hopped about in their hutches. Aimée approached the back door, meaning to pick the lock, but it was not locked. She switched on a small penlight. Once across the hall, she took a few steps into the living room. The thin beam of light from her torch raked the furniture and the drawers that would have to be opened, broken open if need be, so as to suggest a burglary. Then Aimée went back into the hall, took down the Weatherby Regency, and opened it. It was unloaded. She inserted two 12-gauge shells. Cautiously, she went up the stairs. In the second-floor passageway, the bedroom door stood open. The baron's snores were audible.

Aimée entered his room, turned on the lights, and trained the Weatherby's superposed barrels on the baron. At first the light failed to awaken the sleeping man. He lay on his side snoring. His face registered determination.

With the gun still aimed, Aimée continued to contemplate the sleeping baron for thirty or perhaps forty seconds without firing. She frowned. Her lips grew white. She bit them. She seemed to be having difficulty steadying the Weatherby. In exasperation she stamped her foot.

"Fire, for Christ's sake!" she cried.

The baron opened his eyes. Aimée pulled the trigger. She did not see where the spray of shot landed. The baron, clad in striped pajamas, sprang from the bed with an extraordinary bellow. He really sounded like a cow in distress.

"What a hash! Fuck it all!" Aimée was jumping up and down in frustration.

She emptied the second barrel of the superposed. This time the baron was sprayed on the side of his head. Scarlet blood spattered the white wall, trickled into weblike patterns but was quickly absorbed by the plaster, while the man pirouetted, then fell lengthwise with a dull thud onto the bed, where he crouched on knees and forearms. The baron's legs stretched out convulsively, then he pulled them up once more.

13

AIMÉE grimaced, baring her teeth. She let the shotgun fall to the floor, began to pant and then to scream, clutching her head in her hands.

"Stop yelling like that," said the baron.

Aimée immediately fell silent.

"Did I miss you?" she asked in a wondering voice.

"You might say so, yes."

On one side of his scalp the baron sported a red carnation of thick vermilion blood trickling ever more slowly into an eye and down a cheek. Aimée picked up the Weatherby and opened it. The empty shells were ejected automatically. The young woman began to reload. Her gloves, or perhaps her nerves, impeded her. She swore between clenched teeth and sat on the floor to reload more easily. Turning away from Aimée, the baron crawled over to the wall. He managed to get to his feet by clinging to a stack of cardboard boxes containing whiskey, canned pâté, and English cigarettes. Then he let himself slide back down to the floor between the wall and the pile of boxes. Aimée closed the reloaded Weatherby.

"You're not going to finish me off, or are you?" asked the baron.

"I don't know. I really don't know."

Aimée remained silent for a moment, then got to her feet, leaving the gun on the floor.

"I must take care of your wound," she said.

"Calm down. I'm fine. Stay right where you are. I forbid you to come near me!" cried the baron.

Aimée obeyed.

"It's strange that I missed you," she observed. "That has never happened to me before."

"You mean you've killed a lot of people?"

"Seven," said Aimée.

"I was sure there was something," said the baron. "I never thought of that. But I was sure you were special."

"Without counting my husband," added Aimée. She gave a brief chuckle, tossing her head back.

"Bravo, bravo," said the baron. He produced a large soiled handkerchief from his pajama pocket and pressed it to his superficial head injury. He winced.

"With you, it's not working," said Aimée. She took two steps backwards and shook her head in apparent perplexity. "I don't know why but it's not working. I should have known but I just don't know. My God, it's such a muddle, what I'm saying. I'm not going to manage this."

"You do this for the fun of it?"

Aimée shook her head and chuckled again.

"I'm paid for it," she said proudly.

"Who paid you to kill me?"

Aimée shook her head once more.

"I can't tell you. A client is a client. A contract is a contract. I won't tell you a thing."

"Was it Lorque?" hazarded the baron.

"Lorque and all the others," said Aimée. "Lindquist. Sinistrat. Rougneux. Etcetera, etcetera. I have twenty big ones waiting for me in the luggage lockers at the station."

"Twenty big ones?" queried the baron.

"Yes, twenty million old francs. They all paid me. Each one thinks he is the only one. This is my greatest coup. I can retire on it." Aimée burst into tears and sat down on the floor again. "Have I hurt you?" she asked after a moment.

"I'm all right," said the baron.

He was ashen.

"You've gone all white," said Aimée.

"The shock. I'll be fine. I have stopped bleeding. It's just my scalp. It didn't even stun me, so obviously there's no real harm done."

"I am through," said Aimée. "Up to now, this was my thing, you see." She used the familiar second-person pronoun to address the baron. "But of course, you can have no idea." She began to cry again, but softly now. "The first one, my husband, it was a revelation, you can have no idea. I was an idiot, you see. An engineer. I lived with the guy for seven years. A normal guy. In the suburbs, back there." Aimée gestured vaguely in the general direction of the Paris metropolitan area, but perhaps she was referring to some other city. "Just a normal guy," she said again. "Six Ricards a day. He slapped me about. Normal. I didn't feel anything."

She nodded as if to convince herself. Then all of a sudden she recounted how one evening she had grabbed the carving knife from an open drawer. Not that it was the first time her husband had abused her. On the contrary, it had been going on for several years. In any case she grabbed the knife, which was in a rectangular cardboard sheath, and plunged it into her husband's liver without bothering to slip it out of the cardboard. She told the police and the judge that the man had accidentally fallen on the knife. It did not take them long to decide that her account was not implausible. The young judge, who prided himself on his subtlety, found the matter of the cardboard sheath most significant: When you are going to stab someone, he maintained, you bare the blade first. Furthermore, nearly all the fingerprints on the knife were the husband's, for he was the one who always carved the meat or the bird, and who sharpened the knife. (He used to say that the young woman did not know how to sharpen it.) The husband, meanwhile, offered no version of the incident. This despite the fact that it took him ten hours to die. During that time he appeared to be conscious, but he never uttered a word. He seemed detached, and eventually he died. The young woman was not charged.

"It was a genuine revelation, you see," said Aimée to the baron. "They can be killed. The real assholes can be killed. Anyway, I needed money but I didn't want to work."

"Seems reasonable," said the baron.

"Mind you, this is work too, what I do," said Aimée, reverting to the polite form of address. (And her delivery, somehow deadened during her last remarks, now almost completely regained its usual precision and trenchancy, and its rather elegant tones.)

But she appeared to be distracted. She seemed to be looking at the baron but not seeing him. The man was resting his chin on the stack of cardboard boxes behind which he had retreated. His lips were pale and his cheekbones protruded. Aimée gave him a quick summary of her work, telling how she would go from town to town, each time assuming a different personality, and how she would insinuate herself into the most elevated social circles, meaning rich people. And how she observed individuals, and their activities, and the conflicts that invariably arose among them.

"You always end up finding what you are looking for," said the young woman. "There is always one fat real asshole who wants to kill another. The rest is a question of skill. Worming yourself into the client's private life. Putting the idea of killing into his head, where in fact it already is. Then offering your services, ideally at a moment of crisis. I don't tell them I'm a killer. I'm a woman, and they wouldn't take me seriously. I tell them that I know a killer. Sometimes I let them assume that he is my lover. That makes them jealous. It's fun." She sighed audibly. "But now—now it has all gone to hell."

A vague "Huh?" came from the baron.

"From the start, here in Bléville, things haven't been working for me," Aimée said. "I've been wasting time. I didn't know whom to kill. For a moment I thought of suggesting to Sinistrat's old lady that her wretch of a husband could be done in. Or proposing to Sinistrat and his little Julie that old Lenverguez be bumped off. But it was no good. These people are too dumb. It was you who were the ideal quarry, the right target." Aimée swiveled her head vigorously, several times in quick succession. The movement disarranged her blond hair. Wisps of it strayed down over her forehead and the nape of her neck. "But it's no good," she said again. "You hate them even more than I do. You are even screwier than me. I can't kill a guy like you."

"It wasn't viable in any case," muttered the baron. He seemed to be having difficulty holding his head up straight. Being very preoccupied, Aimée did not notice the state he was in. "You can't kill them one at a time," he grunted. "You were bound to stop at some point. Sooner or later you would have been cornered. And even if you weren't. The accepted and established laws are defended against the law of a single individual because they are not empty necessity, unconscious and dead, but are spiritual substance and universality, in which those in whom this spiritual substance is realized live as individuals, and are conscious of their own selves. Hence, even when they complain . . ." The baron paused to cough. A bloody froth had appeared in his nostrils. "Even when they complain of this ordinance," he went on, "as if it went contrary to their own inmost law, and maintain in opposition to it the claims of the 'heart,' in point of fact they inwardly cling to it as being their essential nature; and if they are deprived of this ordinance, or put themselves outside the range of this influence, they lose everything."

"I don't understand a word you're saying and I completely disagree!" cried Aimée. "All I am saying is that I cannot kill a man like you!"

"Right now, perhaps," said the baron with a tired pout. "But your first shot caught me in the upper belly. Shit! What idiocy!" he cried with sudden ire. "You've killed me!"

His head lolled as far as it could. His whole body toppled sideways until it was lying along the wall. Since the piled-up boxes no longer concealed him, Aimée saw that the man's pajamas and the lower portion of his torso were full of holes and covered with blood, and that the baron was dead. The young woman started to get up and go over to the body, but she abandoned the idea and went on sitting where she was, expressionless. She smoked a cigarette.

"You poor old guy," she said at last. "Just wait and see what I'm going to do. Things are going to heat up around here. Just wait and see what I do to them, that bunch of pigs!"

She got to her feet and left the house.

14

"WELL, well, well, my little lady," said Commissioner Fellouque when he saw Aimée. "You're going to break your neck. Where are you off to like that? Is something wrong?"

"I have just killed Baron Jules with a sporting gun," said Aimée.

"My God!"

The dandified policeman drew the back of his hand across his mouth in indecision. He was on the sidewalk with one hand on his car, a Citroën DS21. Despite the biting cold he was wearing only a jacket; in his other hand he held his car keys; the front door of the car on the sidewalk side was open. Aimée had just appeared pedaling like mad, swung in towards the curb, and braked at the last moment; her bicycle had gone into a skid, the rear wheel banging into the sidewalk and the front one fetching up with a slight thud against the bumper of the DS21. The young woman had scrambled off her bike, almost falling to the ground, hopping aside. She let go of the bike, which tumbled onto its side with a clatter. Aimée's face was streaming with sweat. She tried to get past the commissioner and make for the door to the police station, which was fifteen or twenty meters farther on. The man caught her by the upper arm.

"Where are you going?"

"To the cops," Aimée told the commissioner. She shook her head impatiently. "Let me past. Come with me. I'm going to turn myself in. I'm going to confess."

"You are not in a normal state," said Fellouque, keeping a firm grasp on her arm. It was two thirty in the morning. The street was deserted. The tall lamps on low power bathed it in an orange half-light.

"What the fuck is it to you?" Aimée turned to face the commissioner with his large head. "What do you know about this anyway? I'm going to sink the lot of them. I'm going to give them all up. They're rats! Swine! Dogs!"

"Who do you mean?" asked Fellouque.

"They paid me to kill Baron Jules," said Aimée. "So come with me to the police station. I'll make a complete statement."

"But who? Who do you mean?" he repeated rather distantly.

"All of them," answered Aimée, naming a few names and then giving a short laugh. "All of them," she said again. "All those fine gentlemen."

Without releasing Aimée, who seemed to be tottering, Commissioner Fellouque leaned over and reached into the DS21 to get his overcoat. Awkwardly, he slammed the door shut. With his coat under one arm, he pushed Aimée forward but did not let go of her.

"Lorque and Lenverguez?" he asked, repeating two of the names that Aimée had just supplied. "You mean to walk into the Bléville police station in the middle of the night and claim that Lorque and Lenverguez paid you to shoot a man? You must be crazy."

"It's the truth," said Aimée. "Let go of me."

She threw a forearm blow to the side of the commissioner's neck. Fellouque let go of her and fell back. Had it not been for the parked DS21, he would have fallen flat on his back. Leaning against the car, he struggled to get his wind back, wincing, his eyes bulging. Aimée walked towards the police station.

"You are playing into their hands," said Fellouque in a hoarse, very weak voice. Aimée halted. "You just don't understand the situation here in Bléville. You'll be found hanged. Tomorrow morning you'll turn up hanging in your cell." Fellouque was beginning to recover his voice. Aimée had struck him a rather moderate blow. She turned and looked at the policeman uncertainly. "It's the examining magistrate you need to see. Not the station cops. You don't understand anything."

He shook his head and sighed. Grimacing, he bent down to pick up his overcoat, which he had dropped on the ground. Aimée came back to him as he straightened up.

"They have to be picked up right away," she said. She consulted her Cartier watch. "Five minutes from now, that fat Lorque will be waiting for me behind the fish market. Between two forty and four fifteen I have eight appointments. You can pick every one of them up. They will have keys on them, keys to the station luggage lockers. There is money in those lockers. That's your proof. You can nab the lot of them."

Fellouque slipped into his overcoat. He did not button it up, and once again he grasped Aimée by the upper arm.

"First, let's get you inside," he said. His voice was still rather hoarse and he was breathing heavily. "Come." He pulled her along, and she allowed herself to be pulled. "You can give me the details, very quickly. I'll run and scare up the magistrate. Together, the magistrate and I will nab them. Leave it to me. You don't know how things work in Bléville. I do."

At the end of the street, past the police station, Aimée and Fellouque emerged onto the waterfront. Aimée let the commissioner lead her. Her face registered barely any emotion. From time to time she shot a sideways glance at the man, who was walking a step or so ahead of her with his hand behind him, drawing her along after him.

A sole café-bar was lit up and open on the road along the wharves. Fellouque and Aimée went in. It had a narrow frontage and was six or eight meters deep. On the right was a red Formica-topped counter, on the left four red Formica-topped tables in booths with red banquettes. A jukebox stood silent. At the counter, perched on one of three barstools, a drunk in blue worker's coveralls and a peacoat was peering into a Picon and beer as if trying to read the future. A fat man of around thirty-five, in shirtsleeves, sat behind the counter at the cash register, reading the softcover comic-book edition of *Special Operative 117 in Lebanon*.

"Good evening, Commissioner," said the fat man when he saw Fellouque.

"Good evening, lad."

Fellouque steered Aimée into a booth and made her sit. The barman had put down his comic book, come around the bar, and stood deferentially near the booth as Fellouque took a seat opposite Aimée.

"What would you like to drink?" asked Fellouque.

"I'm hungry," said Aimée.

"Do you have anything to eat?" the commissioner asked the barman. "A sandwich?"

"Bread's all gone. I have pastries. Or at least cookies."

"What we don't have is music!" cried the drunk at the counter.

Aimée ordered a beer, Fellouque a Viandox. The fat young man went and busied himself behind the counter. He came back and placed on the table half a pint of Slavia and a large white cup which bore the word "Viandox" in blue letters and held steaming beef bouillon. The left wall of the café was mirrored. There was sawdust on the tiled floor.

"Should I bring the pastries then?" asked the barman.

Aimée shook her head. She was thinking about the baron lying dead in his blood. She had left the lights on in the room where his body lay. The commissioner asked her in a low voice to summarize the situation more clearly than she had done up to now. She summarized.

"As for Lorque and all of them," she said towards the end of her summary, "I gave them appointments to make things sound right. But I was not intending to meet anyone. I have all the keys to the lockers. I made copies. I was planning to catch the four-thirty-five boat train to Paris. Before that I would have picked up all the dough they had left in those lockers. I did the math. It comes to about 200,000 francs. They all wanted me to meet them and hand over the files the Baron had on each of them, and they are supposed to give me their locker key in exchange, but I don't need their keys at all."

"What have you done with the documents?"

"Nothing, I didn't give them a thought. They are back there at the Baron's somewhere. I don't know."

"We'll take care of that later," said Fellouque. "Right now, I am going to see the magistrate. It's best that you stay here."

"If you say so."

Fellouque rose. Aimée stared at the head on her beer; she had not so much as raised the glass to her lips. She half-smiled. Her hair had lost its curl and was sticking to her forehead with sweat. Fellouque gave her an uncertain little tap on the shoulder and went over to the counter.

"Hey, lad," he said to the barman in a half whisper, pointing over his shoulder with his thumb at the motionless Aimée. "Just keep an eye on her. I'll be back. She mustn't leave."

"Got it."

Fellouque returned to Aimée.

"Just don't budge, okay? I'm coming back."

Aimée nodded. The commissioner stood still for a moment longer, then walked very quickly out of the establishment. All of a sudden Aimée gulped down her entire glass of beer, greedily. It left her with a mustache of foam. She wiped her mouth with the back of her hand. She banged the glass on the table and signaled to the barman. The man raised his chin questioningly. She ordered another half-pint and a cognac. He brought them to her. She had emptied both glasses before he got back to the cash register.

"The same again," she called. "And bring me your shitty pastries."

"You like to joke, huh?" said the barman.

"Yes."

"Are you joking?"

"Not really, no."

The man gave up. He brought Aimée another beer and another cognac and shortbread cookies and slices of fruitcake enclosed in cellophane. Aimée stuffed herself and drank. Then she got up and made a run for the toilet at the back of the bar. The Turkish-style john was filthy. Aimée vomited. Around her on the walls were a host of inscriptions, obscene for the most part. *I love sailors with big thighs*, a homosexual who loved sailors with big thighs had written. Someone else had scrawled *Muss es sein?*, doubtless a German tourist, or a German sailor. Aimée remained in the john for a few more moments, not sure whether she was going to throw up again or not. Eventually she came out. Commissioner Fellouque, who had just returned, was standing stock-still in the middle of the dive looking worried. When he saw the young woman he relaxed.

"Come with me," he said. He looked towards the fat barman. "Chalk it all up to me," he said. Then he turned back to Aimée. "Come on," he repeated. "The examining magistrate is waiting for us."

Aimée followed the commissioner, who made for the door. They emerged onto the sidewalk across from the port and braved the damp cold of the night. Fellouque set off towards the bridges and the inner docks.

"Why did you decide to turn yourself in?" he asked.

"I can't do it anymore," said Aimée. "And this time I can take down half a dozen of the real assholes with me."

They crossed the tracks of the railroad that runs the length of the port and started over a bridge. They were headed towards the fish market. This is located, remember, on a sort of promontory flanked by two docking basins, and the pair of moving bridges are attached to the promontory's tip, so that this kind of peninsula constitutes an area accessible from two directions, either across the bridges or, at the other, eastern end, from the mainland of France. Dimmed streetlamps bathed everything in an orange-tinted or perhaps rather a deep coppery light. Aimée spotted DiBona's WSK motorbike in a dark corner in the vicinity of the market. But she did not notice the tobacco-colored Mercedes of the fat Lorque parked in the dirty roadway that runs alongside the market hall, nor the blond Sonia Lorque sitting stiff and tense inside the car. Aimée and Fellouque entered the market precinct.

"Is the magistrate somewhere in here?" asked Aimée.

"What?" responded Fellouque. "Oh, yes, yes..."

He veered towards a warehouse. He and Aimée went inside through an open wicket in a vast door on runners. They were in darkness. Fellouque took Aimée's elbow.

"This way," he murmured. "Careful, there are steps."

They climbed a wooden staircase in the obscurity and emerged into a glassed-in room not unlike a harbor-master's lookout or an airport control tower. Outside, dimmed streetlights were visible on every side, and, much brighter, the dazzling white glare of flood-lights set up here and there along the wharves beyond the docking basins. In the shadows of the glassed-in room several people were standing, at least seven or eight. Behind Aimée, Commissioner Fel-louque closed and bolted the door at the head of the stairs.

"Don't put the lights on," said Lorque's voice, "or we'll be in a fishbowl here."

"Yes, I mean no, okay," said Fellouque.

Aimée took two or three steps into the glassed-in room. She was half smiling, disdainful and weary.

"I was rather expecting this," she remarked in a low voice. The others remained silent. In the yellowish half-light they exchanged embarrassed glances. Commissioner Fellouque was leaning against the bolted door with a detached expression. "It didn't take you long to get together," said Aimée.

"I have a telephone in my car," said Lorque. He took a step to-wards Aimée. He drew his palm across his cheek, the gesture making no sound and thus showing that he had shaved a second time that evening. "You had a pretty good plan. Risky, though. We could eas-ily have spoken to one another and found out that several of us were paying you off. There's a tidy sum waiting for you at the station."

"Two hundred thousand francs."

"Only a hundred and eighty thousand. Our good friend the doc-tor here got cold feet at the last minute."

"I have nothing to do with all this," declared Sinistrat in a high-pitched, quavering voice. "I tried to telephone at one o'clock in the morning to tell you, but there was no answer. I'm not going along anymore. The baron has nothing—he didn't have anything against me, in any case."

"But you were in a blue funk, weren't you, Sinistrat, when you opened that envelope?" came a loud voice that probably belonged to senior manager Moutet.

"It was about an abortion," said Sinistrat. "I don't care if it comes out. In fact I'm proud of it."

"There must be some inconvenient facts in there," grumbled

Lorque. "Medical complications, or money matters. Because it's true, you were in a funk, my dear doctor. And you still are. But that's not the point. The baron is dead because we ordered him killed. We are all in this mess together."

"Not me," said Sinistrat in a stricken voice. "I am merely an observer here."

"Shut up, Sinistrat," commanded DiBona. "You are pissing us off."

"Yes, quite," said Lorque. "Besides, these subtleties are of no concern to Madame Joubert." He took another step towards Aimée. The young woman could clearly discern the features of the fat man with the brownish eyelids. His expression was concerned and sleepy. "I have arranged for the two million old francs you are short to be brought," he said, "and they are here in this room. So you can still take them and go to the station. The commissioner will be delighted to drive you there. You can collect the hundred and eighty thousand francs from the lockers and get on the train to Paris with your plentiful booty. As for the documents, since you didn't take them they are still there at the baron's; the commissioner will have to pay a visit to the scene of the tragic event and take possession of them, then make his initial report concluding that the death was accidental. So even though you have failed to comply fully with the terms of the contract, everything can still be worked out if you wish. But do you wish it? From what I hear, you do not."

A match was struck in the darkness. By its light Aimée saw the calm face of Lenverguez as he lit a cigar. Near the young woman, Lorque remained silent and thoughtful for a moment, his eyes lowered. From the group of men came a cough and the sound of shuffling feet. Having nothing to say, Aimée said nothing.

"In any event," said Lorque, "how can you be trusted now?"

"I can't," said Aimée.

There were two desks in the room, cluttered with papers, along with metal filing cabinets and two chairs. Aimée grabbed one of the chairs, jumped onto a filing cabinet, and, holding the chair out in front of her, leaped through the closed window. She fell from the second story in a shower of broken glass. She landed on all fours; the chair, which she was still holding, shattered into pieces beneath her. A long splinter of wood from the seat broke off and penetrated the left forearm of the young woman, who rolled onto her side, bruising her shoulder and causing the glass fragments beneath her to snap and crackle. She also twisted an ankle slightly.

"Don't shoot, Fellouque!" cried Lorque.

Aimée got to her feet. In the half-light she could see the glassed-in room above, a gaping hole on one side, and the white patches of the faces peering down at her. She wrenched the splinter of wood from her arm and made off as fast as she could, limping a little, towards a dark corner. She slipped into a narrow alley and emerged into the dirty street that runs behind the market. She followed it for some twenty meters, tripping over the piles of empty shells. Then she turned off again down another alley between warehouses. There, in the dark, she stopped and felt herself all over. No bones broken. The glass had cut her superficially on both elbows and one side of her head. Her scalp was bleeding, as was the wound from the wood splinter. But still, she was not losing a great deal of blood. She heard the sound of people running at top speed. At the end of the alleyway where the young woman was lying low two figures passed quickly, breathing heavily, running along the street. Farther away other racing footsteps on the asphalt were audible. After a moment silence returned. Aimée stayed still where she was. She was barely bleeding now. She massaged her painful ankle and her shoulder.

"Madame Joubert?" Lorque called out.

He must have been about fifty meters away. He was not shouting very loudly. Aimée had to listen hard to make out his words.

"We know you are there," he was saying. "You can't get out of this area. We have both ends covered. You can still make a deal with us." The source of his voice shifted, moving farther off. Lorque obviously had no clear idea of exactly where she was. "We are not murderers. It is essential that we come to terms. Answer me!"

The blustering voice continued for a few more moments, less and less intelligibly. Aimée was no longer listening, being taken up with closer sounds. Someone was advancing cautiously down the street, getting close to the entrance to the alley. Aimée groped around silently on the ground. She found and got hold of an empty shell, a large shell, a scallop or the like. Bent double, she crept towards the end of the alley. Against the clear night sky the bookseller Rougneux suddenly appeared in silhouette. For a moment the man peered into the obscurity of the alley, then a flashlight in his hand came on, its beam casting a rather weak light into the shadows.

"She is here!" the man cried in a high-pitched voice.

He took a step back. At the same moment, Aimée stood up straight and, taking three steps forward, struck the man with the shell. Though the shell had not been sharpened, the single blow cut Rougneux's throat.

15

LORQUE was frustrated.

"Rougneux!" he cried in the clear night. "Was that you calling?"

He strained his ears, but no reply came. Lorque was still, his mouth open and his nerves jangled, standing beside his Mercedes. Next to him, the car's left front window, operated by an electric motor, descended silently. Sonia Lorque leaned over and stuck her head halfway through the opening.

"Give me the revolver," said her husband. "Give it to me!" he insisted, when she grimaced anxiously.

Her anxiety unallayed, Sonia rooted in the glove compartment and handed the weapon over. It was not a revolver but a little Austrian 4.25-millimeter pearl-handled automatic. Lorque relieved himself of his nutria fur coat, rolled it up, and stuffed it inside the Mercedes before taking the little automatic and putting it in his pocket.

"Close your window," he ordered. "Don't budge for any reason whatsoever. If you see her, sound the horn."

"Please," begged Sonia. "What are you going to do to her?"

"Close your window," said Lorque again, impatiently.

He glanced west, towards the sea, to the point where the twin bridges led away from the market area. He saw nothing. The various lamps and floodlights of the port gave a deceptive impression of clarity. Indeed the air seemed almost to be filled with a luminous dust. It was not dark at all in the street or on the waterfront but you could not see more than fifteen meters ahead. The humidity must have had something to do with this haziness. Dr. Sinistrat made a sudden appearance amidst the luminous dust. He was covered in sweat. His lips were quivering.

"Have you f-found her y-yet?" he asked.

Lorque shook his head and set off east. He heard Sinistrat hurrying to catch up with him. The two men walked with short lively steps for thirty meters or so down the dirty roadway. Then they came upon a body stretched out on the sidewalk. It was the realtor Lindquist. Lorque and Sinistrat leaned over him. The realtor was dead. He had no visible injuries. Lorque heard the doctor's teeth chattering alongside him and caught the smell of sweat coming off him. Sinistrat switched on a flashlight and played its beam over the entrance, a few meters away, to an alley that connected the street to the quayside. He uttered a tense exclamation when he saw Rougneux's corpse with its throat slit crumpled against the wall at the opening to the alley. Lorque and the doctor hurried over to this second body.

"M-My God!" said Sinistrat. "What did she use to do that?"

"Could have been anything. We've been idiots. She really is a killer. We failed to consider that. She is truly dangerous. Put that thing out!"

Sinistrat complied. The moment the light was switched off, the night's powdery glow seemed more opaque and menacing than ever.

Some fifty meters away, over by the quay, a commotion had broken out because Aimée had just attacked the pharmacist Tobie and her attack had failed in its purpose. The man had taken a notion to open a cold room, thinking, rather idiotically, that Aimée might have hidden there. Coming up behind him, confused by moving shadows, Aimée had bungled an attempted rabbit punch. She had struck too low. Pain flooded the pharmacist's neck, and he fell flat on his face into a pile of fresh fish. He rolled over amidst the fish, kicking, flailing with his fists, and yelling.

"Help! Help!" he cried. "She's here!" Absurdly, he was grabbing fish and hurling them at Aimée. "Wa! Wa! Wa!" he screamed in wild terror.

Aimée delivered a toe kick to his chest; he went quiet and lost consciousness; she bent over him and killed him briskly; then she moved off noiselessly towards the western end of the market area.

A minute later Lorque and Sinistrat, proceeding very cautiously, reached the vicinity of the cold room with its half-open door where Tobie lay dead among the fish. They had come to find the source of the commotion and shouting. They poked around for a moment or two, then thought to look inside the cold room and discovered the pharmacist's body.

"I've had it," declared Sinistrat.

He stood up straight and left at a run.

"Let's stick together—don't be a fool," ordered Lorque, but it was quite useless.

The doctor ran off into the luminescent night and vanished. Lorque withdrew the little Austrian automatic from his pocket and took the safety off. He looked worried but at the same time calm. He went to the middle of the quay and headed east, looking about him frequently. He found Sinistrat lying near a bollard. One of the mooring ropes of a trawler tied up at dockside was wrapped around his neck and had strangled him. As Lorque contemplated the dead man, the rising tide shifted the small fishing boat. The bow of the vessel moved significantly away from the side of the dock. The mooring rope tautened. Sinistrat's corpse was dragged across the quay, then it toppled over the side and fell into the water between the trawler and the wharf. Lorque heard the dead man's skull bumping with dull thuds against the hull of the small craft. Sweating slightly with fear, he continued east. After the killer leaped through the window and disappeared, Lorque had taken charge of operations and dispatched men to both ends of the market area. Now, when he reached the eastern end, the place where the kind of peninsula joined the mainland, he found the two individuals whom he had posted there, namely Lenverguez and the engineer Moutet, dead. Panting a little, the fat man with the brownish eyelids turned and set off to walk back the full length of the area in the opposite direction. He kept to the center of the quay and his finger did not leave the trigger.

He proceeded so cautiously that it took Lorque seven or eight minutes to reach his car. His heart sank when he saw no movement inside the vehicle. He hastened his step. A window rolled down and Sonia's worried countenance appeared. Lorque drew a sigh of relief. His heart was beating wildly in his rib cage.

"You didn't see anything?" he asked.

"No. Did you find her?"

"No."

"She has managed to get away then."

"She had the chance to," nodded Lorque. "Perhaps she did run away. Perhaps not. Perhaps she is still around here somewhere."

"I would almost prefer to think she has escaped."

"Not me," said Lorque.

"What difference does it make?" said Sonia. "You are fifty-nine. You are an honorable man. You have resources. Maybe you'll spend two or three years in prison. Maybe less. I know you, and I know you'll make it. And I'll be waiting for you. I have money put aside. When you get out we'll go to the south. We can end our days in Nice or Roquebrune in peace and quiet."

"No," replied Lorque furiously. "No, I don't want to end up like that. I won't roll over. I'm taking this to the finish and not rolling over." He handed the little automatic to Sonia. "Take this. If you see her, shoot."

"You're crazy!"

"No. She has killed Sinistrat. She has killed Henri. She has... She is absolutely insane and she's a killer. I have to go and see what is happening at the bridge entrance."

"She has what? Henri Lenverguez...?" Sonia swallowed hard. Her eyes widened. "That can't be true, can it?" She shook her head. "I just can't imagine... I could never shoot her, it's absurd."

"Keep that to defend yourself," said Lorque. "I'm going to the bridge."

"Wait!" called Sonia. But her husband was already fading into the powdery glow.

As he passed a warehouse, he hesitated, then went over to a heavy door mounted on runners and opened it by sliding it along its rails.

He switched on the flashlight, which he had retrieved from next to Sinistrat's body. Its powerful beam played over piled-up toolboxes and crates. On a rack hung cargo hooks of the sort used by longshore-men, dockhands, and the like. Lorque grabbed one. Raising his coat behind him, he attached the hook to his crocodile-skin belt at the small of his back. He turned the flashlight off and left the warehouse. He set out again for the bridge. The hook altered his gait slightly.

A delayed reaction to the death of his business partner and the others, and to the mad situation in which he found himself, sparked a sudden surge of emotion in him. He was bathed in sweat. He halted, panting. Mechanically, he rubbed his left arm, where a kind of muscle pain was affecting him. Then he set off once more.

Lorque reached the western end of the promontory. A fog was getting up, pierced by the silhouettes of the moving bridges and the machinery and superstructures needed for their operation. In the open area where the twin bridges met the market area, the roadway, slick with moisture, was deserted. Lorque crouched by a wall. To his left he heard a dull thud, which after a moment of thought he identi-fied: someone had just leaped nimbly from the wharf and landed on the deck of a vessel moored parallel to the market hall. Moving with great caution, Lorque made his way along the quay in the direction of the sound, his neck rigid and his mouth half open. His own some-what labored breathing hindered his ability to hear clearly. From the quay he discerned a figure prone on the deck of a little trawler and another leaning over the first. The leaning figure straightened up. Lorque recognized Commissioner Fellouque. The policeman had a revolver in his hand. Lorque walked along the quay towards him.

"It's me," he hissed. "Did you get her?"

He came abreast of the trawler and with difficulty jumped onto the deck himself. Fellouque seemed stricken. The prone body was DiBona's.

"He's had it," said Fellouque. "He wandered over here to take a piss."

"What an idiot," said Lorque.

Fellouque asked Lorque how things were. Lorque told him that

Aimée had killed all the others. The commissioner found it hard to accept this news. He gazed at DiBona's corpse and shook his head.

"He suggested to me that we leave you to it," he said reflectively. "Just before going off for a piss, he suggested that we let you sort it out with her, you and the others. In the meantime, he wanted us to go the baron's and get the papers, the documents. I said that that was stupid, that she might well make her getaway over a bridge if we didn't keep watch. Then he suggested that I should guard the bridges while he went to the baron's for the documents. He said that the two of us would then be masters of Bléville. It was tempting."

"I bet it was," said Lorque.

Fellouque nodded.

"Well, it's a moot point now." There was a tinge of regret in the commissioner's tone, and of weariness. "Do you really think she is still around here?" he asked, raising his head.

Lorque opened his mouth to reply. A hawser came looping down from the quay above and settled around the commissioner's shoulders. Immediately the hawser tautened and the wire noose tightened about the policeman's neck.

"Oh, no, no!" the man shouted in tones of distress and terror.

Somebody pulled vigorously on the hawser. The commissioner was dragged along, taking a few steps on the trawler's deck before falling between the boat and the wharf. The tension in the cable arrested his descent halfway, just as his lower legs entered the water, which was streaked with fuel oil and full of trash. The man dropped his revolver and it was swallowed up by the water of the dock. He put both hands to his throat. A gurgling sound escaped from his open mouth. Lorque bent down in a frantic attempt to pull the policeman back up, grasping him under the armpits, but just at that moment the hawser unreeled slightly and Fellouque fell completely into the water. Still gurgling, he clung to the trawler's hull and tried to clamber back on board. Lorque held a hand out to him. At the same time, the fat man with the brownish eyelids kept looking up in high alarm at the quay, at the place where the other end of the hawser disappeared in the luminous night. But he could see no one.

Grasping Lorque's hand tightly, Fellouque almost succeeded in getting back onto the fishing boat. But at that instant an electric motor started up noisily somewhere on the quay. The commissioner grasped what was about to happen and screeched in horror. He was done for in any case, for the wire had cut into his neck, and Lorque was aghast to see spurting arterial blood drench the policeman's throat. The power purchase on the quay was now operating. Its cable and the attached wire tensed. Commissioner Fellouque was hoisted aloft, his feet kicking at the air. When he was dangling three or four meters above the trawler, a hanged man with his throat slit, Fellouque's feet stilled and Aimée cut the motor of the purchase. On the double, she left the quay and stationed herself in a room inside the fish market, a room with two exits, one to the quay and the other to the dirty roadway where the Mercedes was standing.

In the darkness the young woman was not visible. Had she been visible, she would not have been beautiful to behold; or perhaps she would have been beautiful to behold, depending on one's taste. She was utterly disheveled. Gummy with sweat, her hair stuck to her skull and fell in damp strands over her brow and the nape of her neck, like the hair of ladies who make love relentlessly for hours at a time. Streaks of coagulated blood varnished her elbows and one side of her head and a whole forearm. Her long wool-knit coat was soiled in places by dust, fuel oil, and fish guts. Her silk blouse was bloodstained, its ribbing slightly torn on one side. Her nose was smudged with dirt. She heard Lorque's voice.

"Let's get it over with!" cried the fat man with the brownish eyelids. "I'm the only one left. Tell me where you are. I'm not going to spend all night looking for you."

By leaning forward a little, Aimée was able, through the door that gave onto the quay, to see Lorque, who had come off the trawler back onto the peninsula and was shouting and wandering about on the concrete with his arms dangling.

"I don't give a shit," he cried. "If you don't tell me where you are, I'm leaving. Perhaps you like playing hide-and-seek. I've had it with this. I'm fifty-nine years old. I'm too old to play around. What happens, happens. Screw it! I'm out of here. I'll spend a few years in prison, big deal!"

He fell silent, waited for a moment, shrugged, and turned on his heel.

"Over here!" shouted Aimée.

Lorque froze. His head twisted this way and that. He was trying to tell where the voice had come from. He massaged his left arm ruefully. He took two or three steps, away from Aimée.

"You're getting cold!" called Aimée.

Lorque stopped again. Turning around right away, he took three long but hesitant strides.

"Getting warmer!" cried Aimée. She chuckled delightedly.

Lorque headed straight for the doorway through which Aimée was watching his approach. He halted once more on the threshold.

"Now you're hot!" said Aimée.

"I am unarmed," said Lorque. "I want to talk to you. Listen here, I don't deserve to die. What have I done except follow the natural impulses of the human race? And even that is saying a lot. We are choirboys compared with our ancestors. Does the sack of Cartagena ring any bells with you? Some of Bléville's bold seafarers were there. I'm not talking about the first sack of Cartagena, that was Sir Francis Drake, but the second, when the French did the sacking. What I've done is nothing alongside the sack of Cartagena. Okay, so I worked a bit on the Atlantic Wall, I had to keep a low profile in South America for a while, then I came back and I've been giving employment to workers and making land productive. I've made my pile in the usual way. Just tell me one outrageous thing, one truly criminal thing, in what I have done, in what the baron had in his files, just name me one!"

"I haven't read the baron's files," said Aimée. Lorque tensed and listened hard, apparently striving to determine the precise source of the young woman's voice. "I couldn't care less," Aimée observed. "Do you really imagine I'm interested in your crimes and misdemeanors? You must be joking!"

Having pinpointed the source of Aimée's voice, Lorque lit his flashlight. Its beam revealed Aimée, sitting and laughing. The fat man with the brownish eyelids reached behind his back and appeared to be rooting in his trousers. Then, suddenly, brandishing the longshoreman's hook, he ran at Aimée with a shriek.

Lorque swung the hook like an ax. Caught short, Aimée was slow to dodge the blow and the hook plunged into her shoulder. At the impact, the handle slipped from Lorque's moist grip. The man fell to one knee as Aimée cried out in pain and staggered against a wall with the hook still buried in her shoulder. Blood spurted; the whole side of her upper body was inundated.

"You asshole! You stinking bastard!" she said. "You've hurt me."

She was tottering. She looked at Lorque, who was still on one knee. He was pale and he was biting his lip. Both his hands were clasped to the left side of his chest. He was short of breath.

"My ticker!" he said. "It's my ticker."

He struggled back to his feet. He made his way to the back of the room, still clutching his chest, still panting and groaning. He went out through the door that led to the dirty street. He seemed to be having great difficulty placing one foot in front of the other. Aimée followed him nonchalantly. Blood was coursing down her whole side as far as her ankle. As she went through the doorway she had to reach out for support and cling to the jamb. She wrenched the hook from her shoulder and threw it to the pavement, where it landed with a clang. The flow of blood increased. Meanwhile, outside, it was possible to tell from the blue tinge to the sky that though the dawn had not yet broken, it would soon do so. Slowly, Lorque made for the Mercedes, dragging his feet. Aimée followed.

"Sonia!" cried Lorque. "Sonia! A heart attack!"

Since he could no longer control his voice, Lorque's words sounded almost boastful, his tone almost triumphant. Then he gave a sharp cry, his knees buckled, he fell on the asphalt, and, rolling over among the discarded shells, died.

Dragging her own feet, Aimée went over to Lorque's body and made sure that the man was dead. The beams of the Mercedes came on. Aimée was caught in the center of their yellow light. Nonplussed, she did not move. She heard the door of the big car open, then Sonia Lorque appeared in the yellow light holding the little Austrian automatic in her hand. The woman advanced towards Aimée. Her cheeks were streaming with tears.

"Is he dead?" she asked.

"Yes," replied Aimée. "He is dead."

"Bitch!" said Sonia Lorque.

Aimée pushed her palms out towards Sonia, as if to repel her.

"I beg you," said Aimée. "I beg you. Please go away. My only quarrel is with the real assholes. I have nothing against you. You do the best you can. It's over now. Please, please, go away."

"But I," said Sonia, "I have things to settle with you. You little shit!" She fired with the small automatic and missed Aimée by a mile. It was a rudimentary weapon, with a very short barrel. Accuracy could not be expected from it. "Couldn't you have left us the hell alone?" Sonia shouted at Aimée. "I don't care what he was. I loved him. I loved him. You damn bitch." Sonia fired again. She was now three meters from Aimée, who was on her knees. The small-caliber round struck Aimée full in the chest. Aimée toppled backwards. The back of her head hit the roadway with a soft thump. "Serves you right, you cow," observed Sonia Lorque. "I loved him, my little guy; I lived only for him." She placed the barrel of the little automatic next to her eye and blew her brains out.

16

THE SOUND of the little automatic resembled the crack of a whip. Sonia took a step backwards, fell against the hood of the Mercedes and bounced off. She tumbled to the ground. Her extremities shook for ten or twenty seconds, then it was over. Nothing moved for about three minutes. It was approximately five past four. Aimée stirred on the ground, then sat up. With her torso erect, straight-backed, she swayed and was obliged to hold herself up with her arms stretched out behind her.

Next to the young woman was Lorque's body; a little farther away was Sonia's. Aimée got to her feet, stumbled over to the Mercedes and turned the headlights off. Through the now-graying night she made out, in one direction, the dock and the trawlers moored there, and beyond them Bléville, where the respectable people slept; in the opposite direction was the other docking basin and, beyond it, the hillside with its working-class suburbs and its streets with names like Jean Jaurès, Gagarin, and Libération. Aimée got into the Mercedes. The keys were in the ignition. She started the car. Her head was continually lolling to one side or falling forward like a dead weight. All the same, she managed to drive away from the market area, over one of the bridges, up the hill through the suburbs where the workers were sleeping FOR JUST A WHILE LONGER, and head north. Blood gummed up one side of her body and clothes. On the other side, the small hole made by the 4.25-millimeter bullet was not bleeding. The young woman seemed to have forgotten the hundred and eighty thousand francs in the self-service luggage lockers and the Paris train. She drove north for seven or eight kilometers, then blacked out for a few seconds, which was long enough for the Mercedes to leave the road. When she came to after her brief syncope, it was too late to straighten up. She braked with all her might, standing up with her foot on the pedal. But at that moment one wheel of the powerful automobile slipped into the ditch, the Mercedes swung across the soft shoulder, skidded in an explosion of grass and earth, and landed up against a tree. The chassis and body were twisted in the middle. Aimée hit her head on a doorframe. For a short while she stayed in the wreck, coughing. Then she got out of the damaged machine. A dirt track led off from the main road about ten meters away. Aimée began walking along it, limping. The dawn was breaking. Aimée's temples throbbed. After a moment, I don't know whether it is part of a vision she had on account of the blood loss or for some other reason, but it seems to me that she was now wearing a splendid, possibly sequined scarlet dress; that there was a glorious golden dawn light; and that, in high heels and her scarlet evening gown, intact and exquisitely beautiful, Aimée was with great ease climbing a snow-covered slope like those in the Mont Blanc massif. SENSUAL WOMEN, PHILOSOPHICALLY MINDED WOMEN, IT IS TO YOU THAT I ADDRESS MYSELF.

—Clamart, Menton, 1976–1977

AFTERWORD

Nine Notes on *Fatale*

THIS IS a *roman noir*, so classified on the back jacket of the French edition, but what *is* a *roman noir*? As we know, the term originally referred to what were also called Gothic novels, a genre initiated in the eighteenth century. Eventually it came to apply only to the type of literature known as crime fiction, a form whose invention, as Walter Benjamin pointed out, coincided with the advent of photography, which meant the end of anonymity in that it made it possible, notably for the purposes of oppression, to identify individuals.

Is the crime novel the kind of novel where death is the prime mover? Where, aside from violence and evil, money is the motor and the stake of the action? Certainly as much may be said of *Fatale*, possibly the darkest of its author's works. Indeed the tone is set as early as the end of the second paragraph, where a group of hunters is presented: "They had been hunting for a good three hours and still had not killed anything. Everyone was frustrated and crotchety." One is tempted to ask whether this mood might not be that of the impatient reader: We have been reading for two paragraphs and still no one has been killed!

This novel is *noir* enough, at any rate, for not a single note of music to make its way in. From Charlie Mingus or Gerry Mulligan in *L'Affaire N'Gustro* to Maria Callas and Bryan Ferry in *The Prone*

Gunman, from Eugène Tarpon's perplexity about Chick Corea to the compositions specifically named in *Three to Kill*, all Jean-Patrick Manchette's other books have musical resonances. There is not a sign of them in *Fatale*. So little sign, in fact, that a drunk who appears fleetingly towards the end of the book in effect deplores the fact. But the darkness of *Fatale* stems above all from the way in which it eschews almost any political statement, whereas as a rule in Manchette's work the political is integral to the organization of the fiction. Here, aside from a few details—the electoral choices of the pathetic Sinistrat, the brisk description of the local newspapers ("one of them championed a left-capitalist ideology; the other championed a left-capitalist ideology"), or the Hegelian and Marxist ramblings of Baron Jules—*Fatale* is devoid of explicitly political content.

Or at least so it seems, for there is a sense in which the project of the heroine, Aimée Joubert, is a political one. A project of the most stripped-down form imaginable: to take money where it is to be found. It is the rich that interest Aimée; she goes only where there is money. In appropriating that money by taking advantage of the contradictions of its possessors, whom she eliminates in the process, she applies a radical and brutal logic which puts the death of the wealthy to profitable use. Curiously, though, despite the strongly utilitarian nature of her murders, she makes a point of clipping and saving the press reports.

On occasion Manchette liked to tell how once, when employed by a publisher to write brief blurbs, he adopted a strict rule: Whatever a work's content might be, he would invariably use the words "sex" and "money" in his description of it. In Aimée's Joubert's definition of her working method (in chapter 7), these two categories, in the same order, are what lead up to the act of killing.

The quantity of victims is impressive. Before Aimée Joubert comes to Bléville, where the greater part of the novel's action takes place, we learn by the bye that aside from her husband, an engineer, she has already killed seven men, among them a factory owner, a stock breeder, and a doctor. In Bléville itself she will eliminate another engineer, another doctor, a pharmacist, an idle nobleman, two more industrialists, and, indirectly, the wife of one of the industrialists. Thus, before her own demise, she clocks up a score of victims drawn from the petty, the middle, and the almost-big bourgeoisie, dispatching them variously by throat-slitting, strangulation, smothering, induced heart attack or suicide, hanging, drowning, stabbing, and shooting with 16-gauge and 12-gauge firearms. All methodically planned and executed homicides; Aimée, who takes care of her own training, has mastered all these techniques. Her targets include not a single member of the exploited classes—not one of those workers who, as Manchette makes clear by using capital letters, as Aimée drives through their suburbs at about four in the morning, are still sleeping FOR JUST A WHILE LONGER.

As so often with Manchette, women are more gently depicted than men. Manchette's men tend to be viewed (and this is especially true in the present work) only under their most repellent aspects. The only touching male character here is the déclassé Baron Jules, who is also the only one with the lucidity to foresee, after fifty pages or so, the end of the story: "You're all done for!" he cries. Indeed. But so is he.

And everyone dies alone. Aimée Joubert has lived alone and will die alone. We know of no earlier relationship of hers except for that with her husband. Twice we see her repel male advances with amusement, and the sole allusion to her sexuality is of an autoerotic kind. She is a solitary figure but a self-transformative one; it is as though she needed to be less alone with herself. For each of her operations, it seems, Aimée changes her appearance, her clothing, or the color of her hair, and she switches the brand of her cigarettes—Celtiques, Dunhills, mentholated Virginia—almost as readily as she does her surname. We see her roles and social attitudes proliferate even though we are never offered the slightest psychological interpretation. On the contrary, Manchette adopts a Dashiell Hammett–like behaviorism, confining himself to the most concrete indications of posture, attitude, or tone of voice. The personality and thoughts of the protagonist must be deduced only from their physical relationship to the world, their material interaction with objects. In Aimée's case this principle is infringed in one respect, twice: the one character trait of Aimée's that is specified is a love of crises, an infatuation with conflict.

Aimée will end badly, of course, and *Fatale*, the last *roman noir* but one to be published during Manchette's lifetime, falling chronologically between *Three to Kill* and *The Prone Gunman*, is first and foremost the account of a defeat. Yet this defeat of a woman seems much more valiant than the defeats of the men portrayed in the other two books. From the closed circle in which the mid-level manager Georges Gerfaut is trapped in *Three to Kill* to the vertiginous yet no less circular fate of the professional killer Martin Terrier in *The Prone Gunman*, Manchette's last two "heroes" rush headlong towards their downfall without hope of any kind. Aimée likewise rushes headlong towards her downfall, yet as she does so she constructs a self, she is engaged in *work*. "Mind you, this is work too, what I do," she tells Baron Jules. And if she has what Martin Terrier calls a "life plan," she will carry it out in a way far beyond the capacities of a Terrier. Of course she fails, and of course her life plan is also a death plan, but her failure is a form of self-realization. And thus the last sentence of the book, which apostrophizes "sensual women," operates at once as an envoi, a warning, and perhaps even an exhortation.

Speaking in an interview of his first encounter with detective fiction, Jean-Patrick Manchette tells what a powerful impression reading Elliott Chaze's *Black Wings Has My Angel* at the age of eight or nine made on him. "The naked girl rolling around in banknotes after the holdup," he says memorably, "was a pretty striking image for a prepubescent kid, and for me it was the 'primal scene' in my development as a *polareux* [a crime-fiction fan]." Later in the interview, Manchette adds: "In the early days of my relationship with my beloved, realizing how knowledgeable she was about crime fiction, I described this scene that I remembered, and asked her did she know where it might be from. 'Sure,' she answered. 'It's from *Il gèle en enfer* [*Black Wings Has My Angel*]. I have a copy.'"

In Chaze's novel this scene, which is indeed startling, occurs quite early on—a "primal scene" that so marked the author of *Nada* that he took it as a kind of novel-matrix to be reproduced and elaborated upon here, in the second chapter of *Fatale*.

It is not common for the name of the main character of a novel to be identical to that of the person to whom the work is dedicated. This is nevertheless the case with *Fatale*, which is dedicated to the person whom Manchette called his *bien-aimée*, his beloved, while its heroine is called, precisely, Aimée. Even though this identity is just one of several that the character assumes as she performs her sinister work, it is by this name that the author for his own part always chooses to refer to her. Manchette obviously has a soft spot for this type of murderess—just as he does, very often, for the other women in his novels: Julie Ballanger, Charlotte Malrakis, Ernestine Raguse, and others, sometimes involved in a certain intimacy with madness, more often entangled with obtuse men. Aimée's first name is meant to be taken at face value: Aimée Joubert loves nobody; that is how she operates, and the only time that she breaks this rule—with Baron Jules—it leads to her downfall. Her method consists in pleasing, in making herself loved before she kills.

Nor is it a common occurrence that an emblematic place-name, invented for the purposes of a novel, should, in reality, have another literary association. Yet this too is a characteristic of *Fatale*, whose action unfolds in a place called Bléville. Rather as with Dashiell Hammett, the reason for this choice is clear: Bléville means town of wheat, of dough, a town where—like everywhere else, but even more so—money rules. And this imaginary port town is where Aimée Joubert comes to practice her art. But it was also in Bléville, in the actual commune on the outskirts of Le Havre, that Raymond Queneau was baptized and later, in May 1914, that he took his first communion. Is there not something poignant about this odd geographical connection between two writers to whom some of us owe perhaps not everything, but almost everything?

"Whichever way you go," writes Manchette, "there is a big hill to climb before you get out of Bléville." In *Fatale*, as elsewhere in Manchette's books, we are liable to find such sentences freighted with strange metaphorical ambiguities. There is another one here too, which leaves us wondering whether it refers ironically to the bloody cleansing undertaken by Aimée or to the moral orderliness required for harmony to reign in Bléville. I refer to a simple injunction, a leitmotif written on weighing machines, public telephones, and municipal wastebaskets: KEEP YOUR TOWN CLEAN!

—JEAN ECHENOZ

TITLES IN SERIES

* *For a complete list of titles, visit www.nyrb.com or write to:*
  Catalog Requests, NYRB, 435 Hudson Street, New York, NY 10014